Praise for Witches

"At once epic and terribly intimate. This is the story of a village, not a city, and all the more powerful for that; not all big fantasy needs an urban setting. Beautifully written, perfectly cruel, and ultimately kind. This is Cornell at the height of his craft."

—**Seanan McGuire**, *New York Times* **bestselling author of the InCryptid and October Daye series**

"Paul Cornell has written a marvelous story, rich in charm, about local politics and witchcraft writ small and personal, but large in consequence. In it he describes the internal feeling of fear and dread far too well, which makes me worry for him, in case he's one of those 'write only what you know' sorts. Coherent magic systems are the acknowledged make-or-break of any fantasy tale, and are all well and good here. You can see the bones of the way magic works in this story, without seeing them tediously spelled out (pardon the pun). But Paul does something else, too, which is perhaps more important and definitely more compelling. He adeptly describes the emotion of magic; its effects and internal ignition of wonder. The feeling of being exposed to magic for the first time and the feel of doing magic and having it done to you have never been better described in any story. This includes, in a fearful little scene, almost terrible in its brevity, the best description of necromancy and its aftereffects I've ever read."

"Masterfully creepy and sinister, all the more so for taking place in the beautifully drawn English countryside."

Also by Paul Cornell

WITCHES OF LYCHFORD

Paul Cornell

A TOM DOHERTY ASSOCIATES BOOK

NEW YORK

This is a work of fiction. All of the characters, organizations, and events portrayed in this novella are either products of the author's imagination or are used fictitiously.

WITCHES OF LYCHFORD

Copyright © 2015 by Paul Cornell

Cover photo by Jay McIntyre/Getty Images
Cover design by Fort

Edited by Lee Harris

A Tor.com Book
Published by Tom Doherty Associates, LLC
175 Fifth Avenue
New York, NY 10010

www.tor.com

Tor® is a registered trademark of Tom Doherty Associates, LLC.

ISBN 978-1-4668-9189-0 (e-book)
ISBN 978-0-7653-8523-9 (trade paperback)

First Edition: September 2015

For the Wonderful Folk of Fairford

Witches of Lychford

1

Judith Mawson was seventy-one years old, and she knew what people said about her: that she was bitter about nothing in particular, angry all the time, that the old cow only ever listened when she wanted to. She didn't give a damn. She had a list of what she didn't like, and almost everything—and everybody—in Lychford was on it. She didn't like the dark, which was why she bit the bullet on her energy bills and kept the upstairs lights on at home all night.

Well, that was one of the reasons.

She didn't like the cold, but couldn't afford to do the same with the heating, so she walked outside a lot. Again, that was only one of the reasons. At this moment, as she trudged through the dark streets of the little Cotswolds market town, heading home from the quiz and curry night at the town hall at which she had been, as always, a team of one, her hands buried in the pockets of her inappropriate silver anorak, she was muttering under her breath about how she'd get an earful from Arthur for being more than ten minutes late, about how her foot had started hurting again for no reason.

The words gave her the illusion of company as she pushed herself along on her walking stick, past the light and laughter of the two remaining pubs on the Market Place, to begin the slow trudge uphill on the street of charity shops, towards her home in the Rookeries.

She missed the normal businesses: the butcher and the greengrocer and the baker. She'd known people who'd tried to open shops here in the last ten years. They'd had that hopeful smell about them, the one that invited punishment. She hadn't cared enough about any of them to warn them. She was never sure about calling anyone a friend.

None of the businesses had lasted six months. That was the way in all the small towns these days. Judith hated nostalgia. It was just the waiting room for death. She of all people needed reasons to keep going. However, in the last few years she'd started to feel things really were getting worse.

With the endless recession, "austerity" as those wankers called it, a darkness had set in. The new estates built to the north—the Backs, they had come to be called—were needed, people had to live somewhere, but she'd been amazed at the hatred they'd inspired, the way people in the post office queue talked about them, as if Lychford had suddenly become an urban wasteland. The telemarketers who called her up now seemed either desperate or resigned to the point of a mindless drone, until Judith, who had time on her hands and ice in her heart, engaged them in dark conversations that always got her removed from their lists.

The charity shops she was passing were doing a roaring trade, people who'd otherwise have to pay to give things away, people who couldn't otherwise afford toys for their children. Outside, despite the signs warning people not to do so, were dumped unwanted bags of whatever the owners had previously assumed would increase in value. In Judith's day . . . Oh. She had a "day" now. She had just, through dwelling on the shite of modern life, taken her seat in the waiting room for death. She spat on the ground and swore under her breath.

There was, of course, the same poster in every single window along this street: "Stop the Superstore."

Judith wanted real shops in Lychford again. She didn't like Sovo—the company that had moved their superstores into so many small towns—not because of bloody "tradition," but because big business always won. Sovo had failed in its initial bid to build a store, and was now enthusiastically pursuing an appeal, and the town was tearing itself apart over it, another fight over money.

"Fuss," Judith said to herself now. "Fuss fuss bollocking fuss. Bloody vote against that."

Which was when the streetlight above her went out.

She made a little sound in the back of her throat, the closest this old body did to fight or flight, halted for a few moments to sniff the air, then, not sure what she was noting, carefully resumed her walk.

The next light went out too.

Then, slightly ahead of her, the next.

She stopped again, in an island of darkness. She looked over her shoulder, hoping someone would come out of the Bell, or open a door to put their recycling out. Nobody. Just the sounds of tellies in houses. She turned back to the dark and addressed it.

"What are you, then?"

The silence continued, but now it had a mocking quality. She raised her stick.

"Don't you muck about with me. If you think you're hard enough, you come and have a go."

Something came at her out of the darkness. She sliced the flint on the bottom of her stick across the pavement and made a sharp exclamation at the same instant.

The thing hit the line and enough of it got past to bellow something hot and insulting into her face, and then it was gone, evaporated back into the air.

She had to lean on the wall, panting. Whatever that had been had almost got past her defences.

She sniffed again, looking around, as the streetlights

came back on above her. What had it been, to leave a smell of bonfire night? A probe, a poke, nothing more, but how could even that be? They were protected here. Weren't they?

She looked down at a sharper smell of burning, and realised that had been a closer run thing than she'd thought: the line she'd scratched on the pavement was burning.

Judith scuffed it over with her boot—so the many who remained in blissful ignorance wouldn't see it—and continued on her way home, but now her hobble was faster and had in it a sense of worried purpose.

It was bright summer daytime, and Lizzie was walking by the side of the road with Joe. They were messing around, pretending to have a fight. They had decided on something they might one day fight about and they were rehearsing it like young animals, she knocking him with her hips, him flapping his arms to show how useless he'd be. She wanted him so much. Early days, all that wanting. He looked so young and strong, and happy. He brought the happy, he made her happy, all the time. A car raced past, horn tooting at them, get a room! She feinted at his flailing, ducked away, eyes closed as one of his fingers brushed her cheek. She shoved out with both hands and caught him on the chest, and he fell back, still laughing, into the path of the speeding car.

She opened her eyes at the screech and saw his head bounce off the bonnet and then again on the road. Too hard. Much too hard.

She woke slowly, not suddenly with a gasp like in the movies. She woke slowly and took on slowly, as always, the weight of having dreamed about him. She recognised her surroundings, and she couldn't help but look over to what, until just over a year ago, had been his side of the bed. Now it was flat, and there were still pillows, pristine, and he still wasn't there.

She found the space in her head where she prayed and she did that and there was nothing there to answer, as there hadn't been for a while now, but after a minute or so she was able—as always—to get up and begin her day.

Today there was a parochial church council meeting. In Lychford, judging from the three she'd been to so far, these always involved whizzing through the agenda and then having a lengthy, intricate debate about something near enough to the bottom of it to make her think that this time they'd get away early. Before this afternoon's meeting she had a home communion visit with Mr. Parks, who'd she'd been called to administer the last rites to last week, only to find him sitting outside his room at the nursing home, chatting away and having tea. It had been a bit hard to explain her presence. Vicars: we're not just there for the nasty things in life. Before that, this morning, she was due to take the midweek Book of Common Prayer service. She looked at herself in the mirror as she put on her crucifix necklace and slipped the white strip of plastic under her collar to complete the uniform: the Reverend Lizzie Blackmore, in her first post as new vicar of St. Martin's church, Lychford. Bereaved. Back home.

The Book of Common Prayer service was, as usual, provided for three elderly people with a fondness for it and enough clout in the church community to prevent any attempt to reschedule their routine. She'd known them all years ago when she was a young member of the congregation here.

"I wouldn't say we're waiting for them to die," Sue, one of the churchwardens, had said. "Oh, sorry, I mean I *can't*. Not out loud, anyway. "Lizzie had come to understand that Sue's mission in life was to say the things that she, or indeed anyone else, wouldn't or couldn't. Just as well Lizzie did little services like this one on her own, except for the one elderly parishioner out of the three whose turn it was to read the lessons, boomingly and haltingly at the same time, hand out the three prayer books and collect the nonexistent collection.

When Lizzie had finished the service, trying as always not to interject a note of incredulity into "Lord . . . save the *Queen*," she had the usual conversations about mortality expressed through concern about the weather, and persuaded the old chap who was slowly collecting the three prayer books that she'd do that today, really, and leaned on the church door when it closed behind them and she was alone again.

She would not despair. She had to keep going. She had to find some reason to keep going. Coming home to Lychford had seemed like such a good idea, but . . .

From the door behind her there came a knock. Lizzie let out a long breath, preparing herself to be the reverend once again for one of the three parishioners who'd left her glasses behind, but then a familiar voice called through the door. "Lizzie? Err, vicar? Reverend?" The voice sounded like it didn't know what any of those words meant, her name included. Which was how it had always sounded since it and its owner had come back into Lizzie's life a week ago. Despite that, though, the sound of the voice made Lizzie's heart leap. She quickly restrained that emotion. *Remember what happened last time.*

She unlatched the door, and by the time she swung it back she had made herself seem calm again. Standing there was a woman her own age in a long purple dress and a woollen shawl, her hair bound with everything from gift ribbons to elastic bands. She was looking startled, staring at Lizzie. It took Lizzie a moment to realise why. Lizzie raised her hand in front of her clerical collar, and Autumn Blunstone's gaze snapped up to her face. "Oh. Sorry."

"My eyes are up here."

"Sorry, only that's the first time I've seen you in your . . . dog . . . no, being respectful now—"

"My clerical collar?"

"Right. That. Yes. You . . . okay, you said to come to see you—"

Lizzie had never thought she actually would. "Well, I meant at the vicarage . . ."

"Oh, yes, of course, the vicarage. You don't actually live here at the church. Of course not."

Lizzie made herself smile, though none of her facial muscles felt up for it. "Come on in, I won't be a sec." She made to go back to the office to put in the safe the cloth bag that didn't have a collection in it, but then she realised Autumn wasn't following. She looked back to see the woman who'd used to be her closest friend poised on the threshold, unwilling to enter.

Autumn smiled that awful awkward smile again. "I'll wait here."

———————

They'd lost touch, or rather Autumn had stopped returning her calls and emails, about five years ago, just after Lizzie had been accepted into theological college, before Lizzie had met Joe. That sudden cessation of communication was something Lizzie had been astonished by, had made futile efforts to get to the bottom of, to the extent of showing up on Autumn's doorstep during the holidays, only to find nobody answering the door. She'd slowly come to understand it as a deliberate breaking of contact.

It made sense. Autumn had always been the rational one, the atheist debunker of all superstition and belief, the down-to-earth goddess who didn't believe in anything she couldn't touch. The weight of being judged by her had settled on Lizzie's shoulders, had made thoughts of her old friend bitter. So, on coming back to Lychford to take up what, when she'd come here to worship as a teenager, had been her dream job, she hadn't searched for Autumn, had avoided the part of town where her family had lived, even. She had not let thoughts of her enter her head too much. Perhaps she would hear something, at some point, about how she was doing. That had been what she'd told herself, anyway.

Then, one Friday morning, when she'd been wearing civvies, she'd seen a colourful dress across the Market Place, had found the breath caught in her throat, and had been unable to stop herself from doing anything except marching over there, her stride getting faster and faster. She'd hugged Autumn before she knew who it was, just as she was turning, which in Lizzie's ideal and desired world should have been enough to begin again with everything, but then she had felt Autumn stiffen.

Autumn had looked at her, as Lizzie had let go and stepped back, not as a stranger, but as someone Autumn had expected to see, someone she'd been *worrying* about seeing. Lizzie had felt the wound of Joe open again. She'd wanted to turn and run, but there are things a vicar cannot do. So she'd stood there, her best positive and attentive look locked on her face. Autumn had quickly claimed a previous engagement and strode off. "Come to see me," Lizzie had called helplessly after her.

Lizzie had asked around, and found that the guys down the Plough knew all about Autumn, though not about her connection to Lizzie, and had laughed that Lizzie was asking about her, for reasons Lizzie hadn't understood. She'd looked for Autumn's name online and found no contact details in Lychford or any of the surrounding villages.

Now, Lizzie locked up, and went back, her positive and attentive expression again summoned, to find Autumn still on the threshold. "So," Lizzie said, "do you want to go get a coffee?" She kept her tone light, professional.

"Well," said Autumn, "Reverend . . . I want to explain, and I think the easiest way to do that is if you come to see my shop."

———————

Autumn led Lizzie to the street off the Market Place that led down to the bridge and the river walk, where the alternative therapy establishments and the bridal shop were. Lizzie asked what sort of shop Autumn had set up. She was sure she'd already know if there was a bookstore left in town. Autumn just smiled awkwardly again. She halted in front of a shop Lizzie had noted when she first got here and stopped to look in the window of. Autumn gestured upwards at the signage, a look on her face that was half "*ta daa!*" and half kind of confrontational. *Witches*, the sign said in silver, flowing letters that Lizzie now recognised as being in Autumn's handwriting, *The Magic Shop*.

"*You* . . . run a magic shop?" said Lizzie, so incredulous that she wondered if the gesture might mean something else, such as "Oh, look at this magic shop, so against everything I've ever espoused."

"Right," said Autumn. "So."

"So . . . ?"

"So I'm sure this isn't the sort of thing you'd want to associate yourself with now that you're a reverend."

Lizzie didn't know if she wanted to hug Autumn or slap her. Which was a pretty nostalgic feeling in itself. "If this is the new you," she said, "I want to see it. I'm happy to step over *your* threshold."

Autumn gave her a look that said "yeah, right" and unlocked the door.

———

Inside, Lizzie was pleased to find herself in a space that said her old friend, scepticism apart, didn't seem to have changed all that much. The displays of crystals, books about ritual and healing, posters and self-help CDs were arranged not haphazardly, but in a way which said there was a system at work here, just one that would make any supermarket customer feel they'd been slapped around by experts. Crystal balls, for example, which Lizzie thought would be something people might want to touch, rolled precariously in plastic trays on a high shelf.

Was there an association of magic shop retailers who might send a representative to tut at the aisle of unicorn ornaments, their horns forming a gauntlet of pointy accidents waiting to happen? She was sure that, as had been the case with every room or car Autumn had ever been in charge of, she would have a reason why everything was as it was.

Autumn pulled out a chair from behind the cash desk for Lizzie, flipped over the sign on the door so it said "Open" again, and marched into a back room, from where Lizzie could hear wineglasses being put under the tap. At noon. That was also a sign Autumn hadn't changed.

"You can say if you're not okay with it," she called.

"I'm okay with it," Lizzie called back, determinedly.

"No, seriously, you don't have to be polite." Autumn popped her head out of the doorway, holding up a bottle. "Rosé? Spot of lady petrol? Do you still do wine? I mean, apart from in church when it's turned into—if you think it *does* turn into—"

"Do you have any tea?"

Autumn stopped, looking as if Lizzie had just denounced her as a sinner. "There's an *aisle* of teas," she said.

"Well, then," Lizzie refused to be anything less than attentive and positive, "one of those would be nice."

Autumn put down the bottle, and they went to awkwardly explore the aisle of teas, arranged, as far as Lizzie could see, in order of ... genre? If teas had that? "So ... this is ... quite a change for you."

Autumn halted, her hand on a box of something that advertised itself as offering relaxation in difficult circumstances. "Look who's talking. You were Lizzie Blackmore, under Carl Jones, under the Ping-Pong table, school disco. And now you're a ... reverend, vicar, priest, rector, whatever."

"But I always ... believed." She didn't want to add that these days she wasn't so sure.

"And I always thought you'd get over it."

Lizzie nearly said something very rude out loud. She took a moment before she could reply. "Autumn, we are standing in your *magic shop*. And you're still having a go at me for being a believer. How does that work? Are you, I don't know, getting the punters to part with their cash and then laughing at them for being so gullible? That doesn't sound like the Autumn I used to know."

Autumn wasn't looking at her. "It's not like that."

"So you do believe?"

"I'm still an atheist. It's complicated."

"You don't get that with craft shops, do you? 'Will this fitting hang up my picture?' 'It's complicated.'"

"Don't you dare take the piss. You don't know—!"

Lizzie couldn't help it. The sudden anger in Autumn's voice had set off her own. "You dropped me when I went away. You dropped me like a stone."

"That was complicated too. That was when things got . . . messed up."

Lizzie felt the anger drain from her. One facet of Autumn's character back in the day had been that she came to you when she needed something. She was always the one who knocked on your door in the middle of the night, sobbing. Had something bad happened to make her come to Lizzie's door again today? "Did you stay in Lychford back then? Or did you go away too?"

"A bit of both." A clenched grin.

"Where did you go?"

Autumn seemed to think about it. Then she shook her head. "I shouldn't have come to see you. I'm sure you're busy, Reverend, I've just got to . . ." She gestured towards the inner door. "You see yourself out."

Lizzie desperately wanted to argue, but just then the shop bell rang, and a customer entered, and Autumn went immediately to engage with her. Lizzie looked at the time on her phone. She needed to go to see Mr. Parks. "If you need me, Autumn," she called as she left, and it was on the verge of being a yell, "you let me know."

———————

The following evening, Judith decided to do something she had never deliberately done before. She was going to participate in the civic life of the town. Which meant that first she had to negotiate getting out of her house. She went to put the recycling out, having spent a relaxing five minutes crushing cans with her fingers, and found that her neighbour, Maureen Crewdson, was putting hers out too. Maureen had found herself running for mayor, unopposed, because nobody wanted to do it. "By accident," she'd said, having one night had a few too many Malibus down the Plough. Of all the people Judith had to put up with, she was one of the least annoying. She had, tonight, the same weight about her shoulders that Judith had seen for the last few weeks. "I'm coming to the meeting tonight," Judith told her, and watched as, imperceptibly, that weight increased.

"I didn't think you'd be bothered with all that. Are you for or against the new shop?"

"I've decided I really don't like it." Since summat had had a go at scaring and then attacking her for considering voting against, that was.

The weight on Maureen's shoulders increased again. "Oh. It's going to bring so many jobs to . . . sod it, can we please not talk about it?"

There was some strangling emotion wrapped around her, something only Judith could sense, that would take a bit of effort to identify. Judith didn't feel up for poking into her business that much at this point. She knew better than to go rummaging into private pain. Looks like it's going to rain, dunt it?" Judith felt the relief as she left Maureen to it, and went back inside to make herself a cup of tea while considering her exit strategy. She waited until a few minutes before she had to go, then took a deep breath and called up the stairs. "I'm off to the meeting." Silence. That was odd. What had happened to the noise from the telly? "Arthur? You hear what I said?"

This silence had something aware in it. Mentally girding her loins, Judith set off up the stairs.

———

Arthur was sitting where he always sat—in the bedroom, in his favourite chair, which he'd had her haul up here, the sound of his ventilator sighing and heaving. It was normally obscured by the constant noise of the telly, but the mute was on, and Arthur was fiddling with the remote, trying to get the sound back. He was watching some quiz show. That and ancient whodunits were all he watched, the older the better. Judith kept the Sky subscription going just for him. He didn't acknowledge her arrival. "Arthur, I said—"

"I heard you, woman. You're leaving me again."

She didn't let her reaction show. "It's only for an hour, and your programme's on in a minute." *Waking the Dead.* He loved gory mortuary dramas. Of course he did. She took the remote off him and tried to find the button to unmute it, which was hard in this light.

He looked up at her with tears in his eyes. "You'll be sending me away soon. Your own husband. You'll be putting me where you don't have to see me."

"If only I could!"

His face contorted into a sly grin, his cheeks still shining. "Will your boyfriend be there tonight, full of Eastern promise? Oh, that accent, he's so lovely, so *mobile!*"

She kept on trying to work out the remote, not looking at him. "You don't know what you're talking about, you old fool."

"That'd make it easy to send me away, wouldn't it, if I was going mental? You reckon he can make you feel young again? You're planning to get rid of me!"

"I bloody can't, though, can I?" Judith threw the remote at somewhere near him, turned on her heel and marched out of the door, only for her conscience to catch up with her, along with his howls of laughter, on the first step of the stairs. With an angry noise in her throat, she went back in, managed to switch the sound back on, slapped the remote back into his hands, and then left the cackling old sod to it. She put on her coat. As she got to the front door she heard his laughter turn to stage sobs, or real sobs, but still she made herself get outside and close the door without slamming it behind her.

2

The town hall was packed. A table had been placed at the front of the stage, under the Union flag and the Gloucestershire coat of arms. Displays on easels to the left and right showed artists' impressions of Lychford with a new superstore at the heart of it, lush greenery surrounding it, children playing and adults waving to each other outside it. Judith looked around her awkwardly, aware that she'd had various issues in the past with several of the locals who'd gathered here to voice protests against the store being built. She caught the eye of Eric and Sheila Parker, the couple who'd led the anti-superstore campaign on Twitter and had leafleted the town about it. They were here in matching "Stop Sovo" T-shirts. Judith realised, with horror, that they were heading over to talk to her, and couldn't find, at a quick glance, anyone else she knew well enough to get into a conversation with. There were, just occasionally, drawbacks to being a nasty old bitch.

"Judith!" called Mr. Parker, reaching out both hands as if to hug her. "You've seen the light."

"You could say that."

"I can't believe Sovo's gall, trying again," said Mrs. Parker. "This is how all the supermarket chains do it. Lose the first public vote, work out what they can bribe the locals with, win the appeal. This meeting is the bribery part of the process. The council votes next week."

"How are 'our side' doing?" asked Judith, wincing silently at having used the verbal speech marks. She never could force herself to bloody *join* anything. From the look of the crowd in the room, divided very cleanly in twain, each side having sat with those who agreed with them, the feeling of the town was about evenly split.

"I think we're going to win. Just. Every vote counts."

Maureen, looking just as burdened as earlier, walked up onto the stage and took a moment to prepare her papers. "Ladies and gentlemen," she said, "I'd like to introduce you to David S. Cummings, Chief Executive in Charge of New Development, Sovo Superstores International. I hope you'll give him a fair hearing."

A heavily built man with strong shoulders and nice eyes, dressed in a very expensive suit, took to the stage. There was a mixture of applause and catcalls.

"That's their fixer from head office," whispered Mrs. Parker.

"We've heard the bribery has become literal," said Mr. Parker. "The word is that the mayor has taken some sort of backhander."

Judith realised, with a sudden ache in her chest, that now she understood what she had felt around Maureen. She made the effort to look more closely, as only she could, and found weakness and fear and betrayal caught in the folds of the mayor's cardigan like smoke. Maureen looked up from her papers and made eye contact with Judith and the conflict in her eyes confirmed everything. Judith had to turn away, and found she was looking at Shaun, her son, in his uniform. He was pointing at her in surprise.

"You're here. You've taken a side."

"Yes."

"Because I was very much hoping—"

"That I wouldn't."

"Just so we're clear—"

"I won't throw anything."

"See that you don't. I don't want to have to arrest you. Again." He pointed to his eyes and then to her, and, with another glance at her over his shoulder, marched back to his place at the back of the hall.

Judith found a seat next to the Parkers as Maureen brought the meeting to order. She made a few more words of introduction, then gave the floor to Cummings, who stood and held out his hands, palms up, asking for the audience's indulgence. There were again boos and cheers in response. He smiled. "Being booed in a town hall. Now I've really made it as a pantomime villain." His accent was middle class, straight down the middle. "Good evening, everyone, your honour, councillors. Sovo are back here, having opted to go through the appeal process, because our research indicates fifty percent of you *want* us to build a store in Lychford."

"And half of us don't!" called Mr. Parker.

"The town council, I'm sorry to say, are also split down the middle. So, as most of you will be aware, next week they're going to put this to a final vote."

"You're tearing this town apart!" yelled Mr. Parker. Mrs. Parker put a hand on his arm, but he shook her off.

Cummings gestured towards a flipchart. "We've heard your concerns and adjusted our plans. I hope the changes may persuade a few more of you towards our point of view. We aim to meet challenge with investment. Investment in people. The creation of over two hundred new jobs. Yes, our new facility would change the shape of Lychford. But we hope it's for the better." He turned the first sheet, and revealed an even more lovely painting of an idyllic store in local surroundings. Below it was a more detailed map.

It took a moment for Judith to understand what she was looking at. She took her glasses from her pocket, stuck them onto her nose, and stared at what had been revealed. She had wondered if there was any connection between the fleeting poke of mystical energy she'd run into and the proposals about the store, but she'd never imagined *this*.

"By diverting these roads," Cummings indicated on the map, "the proposed new store would actually bring *more* traffic to local businesses."

Judith suddenly found she was on her feet. Beside her, the Parkers grinned and urged her on. "You'll cut off Compton Street?"

"Yes, and that will mean—"

"That the streets don't cross at the Market Place!"

"Which is why we'll be building, free of charge, a new Market Place parking zone—"

"You bloody fool!" shouted Judith, before she could help herself. "You'll open the gates to the other worlds!"

There was silence, followed by a little awkward, embarrassed laughter. Judith heard, from the back of the hall, Shaun make a little groan of anguish.

She looked down to see the Parkers staring up at her in amazement, but she had her opportunity, they were listening to her, she couldn't stop now. "This town is shaped like it is for a reason! The roads, north south east west! The walls that protect us, seen and unseen, follow that pattern, use it as their foundation! The ancient boundaries, our defences—!" She could hear both sides of the audience starting to catcall now, shouting for her to sit down. She'd actually united the town in something. But she had to say this, they had to know, it was so important. "We've already lost the tree line on Maiden Hill—"

"That was kids playing with bonfires!" hissed Mr. Parker. "For God's sake, sit down!"

"There'll be nothing to stop it! Don't you understand? I understand now why I felt something trying the defences! If you do this, then the things that are out there, that want to get in—!"

The doors to the hall burst open. A great wind blew leaves in and sent papers flying. There were screams. Everyone, Judith included, turned, to see a figure standing silhouetted against the streetlights outside. The figure halted, seemed to realise that he'd made a big entrance, and turned to grab the doors and heave them closed behind him. He was, his actions revealed, a thin, long-haired youth in a leather jacket. He turned back to the crowd and looked awkward. "What?"

Relieved laughter swept the audience. Judith looked helplessly around her. The moment had been lost.

Cummings was watching her, sizing her up, obviously wondering how dangerous this lunatic was. "I'm sure," he said, "that this lady's views are something we all want to give ... *appropriate* consideration to." Which made the audience laugh once again.

Judith sat down, lost.

_____

She made it through the meeting, despite the Parkers hissing icy comments at her, and then had to head for the door—away from where Cummings was shaking Maureen's hand, away before more people could tell her what a stupid old woman she'd been. They were right. She shouldn't have blurted it all out like that, should have found some reasonable way to say it. If she knew people here better, if she'd had some more friends to call on—! Stupid old woman, stupid! Shaun intercepted her before she got to the door. "Mum, it's okay."

"No it isn't, boy. It isn't for any of us."

"Oh, thank you so much for that, Judith." Mr. Parker caught up with her. "Use a spell and magic this away, won't you? You made our case look ridiculous!" The horrible thing was, he was right. At the end of the meeting there'd definitely been more applause for David Cummings than abuse.

Shaun stepped up to him. "See you later then, Mr. Parker."

After a moment he took the point and marched off, finding his wife. They, and many others, gave Judith baleful glares as they headed out.

"Thank you, people who don't understand

metaphor." Judith turned at the welcome sound of the new voice, to find Sunil at her side. He was smiling in his usual wry, understanding way. He was wearing his spectacles tonight, which, she knew, would have been a big decision for this handsome seventysomething man who took such good care of himself. She reflected again that there were just a few things about which Arthur was entirely correct. She appreciated Sunil's support, but she really didn't want to have this conversation with him now. Still, she let him take her arm and escort her to the door.

———————

PC Shaun Mawson had become aware at an early age that his mum believed in some weird stuff. Not that she'd ever shared the details of it with him. He'd asked about the details several times and been told he couldn't know about it because he was a boy. Judith's reputation for fearsome confrontation had helped him through school, where the teachers had seemed as nervous of her as his classmates were. As an adult, with her getting on a bit, he'd gotten increasingly fearful that her mouth might one day get her into something she couldn't get out of. So it was with a sense of relief that he watched her leave the hall. He wasn't sure what he thought about Sunil taking her arm in public like that, mind you. Yet another reason for people to talk about Mum. His thoughts were interrupted by a hand grabbing his shoulder and spinning him round. He found he was facing the long-haired stranger whose dramatic entrance had caused such laughter, who was now appraising Shaun with a piercing stare. "You know her, don't you? Tell her well done for having a brain. She's the only one who talked any sense." His accent was hard to place, perhaps Irish, perhaps the sort of cockney who'd been in America too long.

"Very kind of you, sir, now we're trying to empty the hall . . ."

The man made a guttural sound at him, then marched off into the crowds that were flooding past, trying to stop and persuade them. "Why didn't you listen to her wisdom? Damned *people*! Don't you value your short little lives?" Which Shaun didn't like the sound of, but when he tried to catch up with the man, he found he'd lost him in the crowd.

———

Sunil walked with Judith through the quiet of the car park. She was heading back towards his car, she realised, without either of them having commented on or thought about it. His concern didn't annoy her, which was unique. He was someone in this town who wanted to understand her, who even liked her, and that was unique too. After a moment they were alone under the trees by the bridge, at his car, with no bloody Parkers or anyone else to see them. Judith let out a long breath of relief. She'd only just realised, but she was still so angry and frightened for the future that she was shaking. She found she was hoping Sunil might put an arm round her, but no, he was far too decent to do that. "If only they'd under-stood," he said, "as you say, the shapes of things are important. When I start a new business, I look at demand, at where the customers are—"

"Oh, stop being so bloody kind. You know I meant it literally."

"I know you believe in . . . well, I don't know what the proper name for it is, but such seriousness is fascinating. How about you tell me everything? Over dinner tomor-row night, say? Not at my restaurant."

"Why?" She couldn't help teasing him. "Is it the food?"

"Because my staff would laugh at me, being on a date." That twinkle in his eye. Here it was, a specific invitation. He'd never previously gone that far.

She had both hoped for and dreaded this moment. "Sunil, you're very nice, but . . ." She didn't want to finish the sentence, to say out loud that she just couldn't do this.

He sighed. "You still have your whole life ahead of you. Please, think about it." He very gently touched her arm, and smiled supportively again, and went to his car. Judith watched him drive off and thought about what could never be and then swore at herself for doing so. She had to drive such thoughts from her mind. It was time for battle.

———————

The next morning, having unlocked the church, Lizzie found herself pausing at the point where she normally bowed in front of the cross on the altar. Mr. Parks had been once again surprisingly full of life at his home communion, but had said *she* seemed off her game. She hadn't slept. She was still so angry at Autumn. Had she come back home hoping for the relief—a reconciliation with her best friend? She so much wanted to tell her about Joe, about his death, about her own part in it. Everyone at the time had been so quick to tell her it was an accident. She and Joe had been caught on CCTV camera, she'd been told, though she hadn't wanted to see it. The police had—horribly quickly—cleared her of blame. Maybe what she really wanted was for unpersuadable, sceptical Autumn to listen, to ask questions, to believe her. That

Autumn, though, would never have owned a business she didn't believe in. That Autumn would never have said anything was "complicated."

Maybe Lizzie was stuck now. Stuck here, with no faith in her head, no relief. She'd alienated her best friend years ago, and killed the love of her life, and couldn't bring herself to ask for help, because maybe she was committing the sin of not thinking she deserved it. "Oh, what's the bloody point?" she said out loud. She looked from the cross to the beams in the ceiling. "Is there anybody there?"

There was a sudden noise from behind her. Lizzie spun, to see that a man had entered the church and was looking at her apologetically. "Sorry. Only me, as they say." He extended a hand. "Dave Cummings. You may have heard. I'm the man from Sovo."

"Oh. Hi." Lizzie managed to control her breathing.

Cummings wandered further in, looking around at the architecture. "Oh, dear no," he said, "it'll have to go." He saw her startled reaction and laughed. "Joking. Sorry, I always assume that's what people imagine I'm thinking, wherever I go in this town. I'm the Antichrist."

"I'm strictly agnostic about all that," Lizzie assured him. "I have to get on with everyone." In truth, the battle lines had been drawn before she got here, and she could see good points on both sides, and apart from caring for those involved, it wasn't a conflict she was much invested in.

"It's actually a lovely church. Cotswold stone, tower in the perpendicular style, all funded by wool merchants, but built around a considerably more ancient original, am I right?" He saw that he was, and was pleased with himself. "Excellent. Could do with a rood screen, most churches round here once had them, very few left. Font and pulpit placed a bit awkwardly for everyone to see. Oh, you must have thought of that, I'm teaching my grandmother to suck eggs. I hope we can bring more people in here."

"Oh? Is that something your company are into?"

"Well, it's part of the fabric of British life, isn't it? A bit like we are, these days. Community, reliability, together-ness. All very pleasing. Sovo head office donates to a lot to Christian groups."

"I'll take your money. We have a local charity that runs a food bank."

He raised a hand to urge caution. "Such donations being facilitated through organisations like Only Way and the Truth and Light Alliance."

"Ah." Those names meant, to Lizzie, a very particular brand of extremity.

He must have seen her expression. Her attentive and positive face was utterly beyond her at the moment. "Not your sort of people?"

"It's just they're rather more . . . controversial . . . than—"

"Oh, I'm sure they'd say the same about you. It's a pity you judge them and find them wanting. I thought you might want to get some real energy in here, change things around. It's all a bit . . . quiet."

Lizzie wanted to say he should see it on a Sunday morning, but she was trying to find an appropriate manner of speech. He'd caught her at exactly the wrong moment.

"Or perhaps you like the quiet? Like it being just you? Gives you time to think, I suppose. Lots of time alone to dwell on . . . well, whatever."

Did he know something about her? "Why are you talking to me like . . . ?"

"Like what?" He looked suddenly concerned.

"Nothing. Sorry."

"Have I said something to offend you?"

"No," she decided. "No, I think . . . sorry, we seem to have got off on the wrong foot."

"No, no, it's my fault. You mentioned your food bank . . ." He went over to the collection plate that last night's youth service had left out on the side altar, reached into his pocket, and placed on it an enormous wad of cash. "There."

Lizzie was too astonished to say anything.

"See you again soon, Reverend," said Cummings. He headed for the door.

Lizzie waited for a decent moment after he'd left, then went and stared at the roll of fifty-pound notes. There was enough there to keep the food bank charity going for . . . well, years. She hadn't even said thank you. She reached out with the aim of taking the elastic band off the money, to count it, to get it into the safe as quickly as possible, but then she stopped.

For some reason she didn't understand, she couldn't bring herself to touch it.

———

Autumn had resolved to open the shop on time, despite her lack of sleep. She'd had quite a few customers in over the last few days, ones she hadn't met before, all of them, it seemed, seeking specifically or including in their orders ingredients that were supposed to be able to allow one to hide or vanish. It was as if the New Age community in this and the surrounding towns was bigger than she'd thought and was preparing for some sort of conflict. Their grim faces and refusal to engage with her careful counselling about the proper uses of what they were buying matched her mood. She didn't believe they were actually capable of changing the physical world with what she sold them—that lack of belief was the bedrock of who she was—but from all the years of research she'd done into magic, she knew the rituals they were about to enter into had meaning for the customers themselves, could change who they were. She'd tried, when she couldn't sleep, her own rituals about calmness and sanity, to no avail.

As she unlocked the cash register, her hands fumbled angrily with the keys. Why had she bothered to go and see Lizzie? What had she expected to get out of that, exactly?

All those years ago, her friend had announced out of the blue that she was taking up a major role in a belief system responsible for so many horrors, and when Autumn had paused, needing time to think about this sudden enormous change, Lizzie had started sending her passive-aggressive emails, demanding Autumn answer. Then . . . well, then had come the moment when everything had fallen apart.

Maybe Autumn had gone to see her hoping she could share what had happened, hoping she'd understand, Lizzie being a professional believer. Maybe Autumn had thought she might see her story in a way that Autumn herself couldn't. That look on Lizzie's face, though, that had told Autumn she could never understand the atheist owning a magic shop thing, never mind the . . . the cause of that seeming contradiction. Her going to find Lizzie had been, she decided, the result of desperation, her reaching out for old comfort that wasn't there any more, in the face of . . . a threat which wasn't real, which couldn't be real.

Autumn realised she could hear something again now. In the same instant she went through what was now a familiar process—thinking what she was hearing was just in her awful memories, but then realising that it wasn't.

It was music, or something like music.

A couple of years ago, she'd made herself learn enough musical notation to attempt to write it down, but even then she'd failed. It was a high, repetitive, six-note strain, followed by a recurring three-note sound that seemed like a . . . summons, that circled, floated, repeated, pure liquid sound.

She'd read many accounts of people who claimed to have heard the same sounds, and some of them had such good explanations of what it might be: wind blowing through gaps in stone, shifting quartz scree, even the sound of killer whales through the canvas hulls of boats. None of those could explain why this sound she associated with a horrifying period of insanity had returned, a couple of weeks ago, right outside her shop.

Her hands started shaking uncontrollably, and she dropped the keys. She put a hand to her mouth, looking around wildly, trying to find the threat that might come from any direction. It was coming this time, she realised, from just behind the back door.

She forced herself to walk, step by shaking step, towards the sound. Was it him? As if she was sure there had *been* a him. She had struggled so long with what she'd started to see as mental illness. Now she was closer to the door, she could hear it clearly: the same music that had been blaring into her ears in the chamber of his . . . his father. She shook her head, trying to push the memories, the stories she'd told herself, the symptoms of her illness, whichever, out of her mind. She was looking at the frosted window at the back door. A shape stepped forward. There was someone . . . something there.

Then it was gone.

Autumn had blinked, and perhaps there'd been a blur of movement, perhaps not. At least the music had stopped. Only then . . .

. . . she slowly turned. It was coming again, this time from near the front of the shop. She closed her eyes, and could only find images from the past, or from her imaginings, crowding in on her. Her walking hand in hand with . . . him . . . no, *it*. The clearing in the forest to the east of here—he'd led her into it, and she'd been so amazed to see the line of flowers strung between the two enormous trees. That music had been everywhere, lighter then, inviting. In her memory, she could taste it somehow in the air. He'd raced towards the bower, gesturing happily for her to follow. She'd hesitated on the edge of the two trees, struck suddenly by what deep shadows they cast. He'd come back round behind her, put a hand on her shoulders and had suddenly . . . pushed her—

She didn't want to remember anything after that. It was impossible. It was *all* impossible. Lizzie was saying all the time with her bloody collar that she knew everything about what happened in heaven and earth, only that didn't include what had happened to her, to Autumn. The music was getting louder, or was that just in her head? "You're not real," she whispered, "you're not real."

After a while, the repeated words seemed to work. The music faded again. Then it was definitely gone. Autumn was left shaking. She thought of Lizzie, thought of running back to that damn church, into it . . . but no. All the learning she'd done, all the research . . . perhaps it had all been to deal with this moment when she came to question her sanity again. She had to find some way to protect herself.

3

Judith had decided to check on all the ancient boundaries, so that lunchtime she had her usual going-out row with Arthur, before making her way to the Market Place, then up the street that led eastwards out of it. This had traditionally been the way sheep had come from the hill farms into Lychford on market day.

The dry stone walls along the way weren't in a good state of repair, but as the houses gave way to the edge of the forest, they didn't look like they were going to fall over any time soon either. These stones had been laid with care by those who knew that all the old crafts had a hidden dimension to them, that the placing of a bonder stone changed everything.

Out this way there was the lonely last pub, the Castle, which now had an angry chalkboard sign up that said "drinkers welcome" to indicate its dissatisfaction with other establishments' fads like pub quizzes, bands, food, and, presumably, conversation. Beyond it the road got dark, but that was where the darkness was supposed to be.

Judith looked up at a noise and saw that an enormous Sovo lorry was approaching, cutting through Lychford when traffic was light rather than using the bypass, she presumed, on its way to deliver to a Sovo store in any of a dozen nearby towns. However, as it roared past her, she heard another noise, and watched as the stone in a section of the wall shuddered, a couple of "batter" stones from the top falling away. Furious, she grabbed one of them, turned and flung it helplessly after the lorry.

Which it missed by a mile.

Hopefully the driver had at least registered, in his rear-view mirror, her impotent protest. These people were such fools, they had no idea what they were risking. She raised her index and little fingers at the driver, just so he got the point. Then the lorry was gone around the corner. To Judith's surprise, a car following it skidded to a halt and out of it sprung Mr. Parker, his face florid. "What the hell are you doing now?" His wife was getting out behind him, looking more worried than angry. "Did you really just make a . . . magic sign at that lorry? After throwing something at it? It all gets reported back to head office, you know. You should see some of the stories they've planted in the local media. It's going against us now. We're actually losing support. Thanks to you!"

Mrs. Parker caught up with her husband. "Eric, please don't—"

"How dare you make a laughing stock of us? After all I've done!" He poked his finger into Judith's face.

Judith, not used to being lectured by the middle-aged, had glanced away, back to the wall, and what she'd seen there had made her afraid in a way Eric Parker never could. Standing at the edge of the woods, by the now slightly diminished wall, was an extraordinary figure. It had the shape of a man, but was almost a silhouette, a few lines of a sketch, stark white against the shadows of the trees beyond. It had no features, and yet Judith knew it was looking at her. It took a purposeful step forward.

Eric Parker and his wife stepped forward in that moment too, as a passing car made them get out of the road. "Look at me when I'm talking to you!"

"Eric, for God's sake!" Sheila was getting scared for reasons unconnected to the thing only Judith could see.

Judith looked back and called desperately to the figure. "You can't get in. Not yet. No matter how strong you are. Go! Now!"

Mr. Parker shoved Judith right up against the remains of the wall, sending another stone falling from it. "No, I won't just do what you say because you're magic, you ridiculous old cow! Have you thought about supporting the other side? How about making them look stupid too?"

Judith looked back again to where the figure, now

inches away, was regarding them all calmly, purposefully. She caught a familiar scent. This was a more physical form of the probe she'd felt from one of the worlds beyond the borders. Creatures like this were rarely seen in the world of people. Surely it should take longer for them to become this confident?

"Oh, is there something there we can't see? Are the voices talking to you again?" Parker grabbed the collar of her coat, making Sheila cry out for him to stop. Judith raised her stick, against which threat she wasn't sure. She twisted and saw the figure consider for a moment. It reached out.

Its hand slapped onto Mr. Parker's shoulder. He spun at an impact he could obviously feel, and his expression contorted into shock as, suddenly, he could *see* it too. The figure let go. Mr. Parker stumbled back, his face suddenly flushed. His hand dropped from Judith and grabbed at his own chest.

"Eric!" shouted Mrs. Parker. "Eric, where are your pills?"

Judith looked back again. The figure was holding something between thumb and forefinger: a bottle of pills.

The damn demon! Judith made a grab for it, but the intruder had already stepped back. As Mr. Parker fell and Mrs. Parker started screaming, knowing that now Judith didn't dare clamber over what remained of the wall and follow, it calmly walked off into the trees and was gone.

———————

Judith tried, though she had no knowledge of first aid, to help. She yelled at Mrs. Parker to call 999. Shaun, of course, was first on the scene, and he kept up heart massage on the utterly still Mr. Parker until the ambulance got there. All Judith could do was hold Mrs. Parker's hand, which she accepted, sobbing. As the Parkers were driven away in the ambulance, Shaun looked concerned at her. "There wasn't anything more you could have done, Mum."

"No," muttered Judith, looking back to where the wounded wall still stood, a breach that would take more than a simple replacing of bricks to fix. "That's the trouble."

———————

Autumn had spent the morning checking her shop's defences. She'd chosen which empty shop to rent on the basis of its proximity to running water. She'd salted every threshold, had buried witch bottles and the treated bones of cats in holes she'd dug in the supporting walls. As she'd done all that, she'd said the incantations that focussed all one's consciousness on protection. Now she went back to those defences, said all those calming words again. She did not believe, she told herself, in the power of the objects, or that she was changing the physical world, but instead that she setting up the shop/fortress as a metaphor in her mind, hacking her own brain to withstand the possibility of a relapse. The music was a symbol of mental illness, and she could use her own symbols against it.

She did honour to the four compass points, raised the three forms of the goddess within her, as she'd done hundreds of times over the last few years, and found some slight calm in the familiarity of the ceremony. She had chosen, all those years ago, to investigate that which had harmed her, to understand it and encompass it. She fought her mental illness on its own territory. Now it was early afternoon, and her serotonin levels would be low, and, as she thought she might, she thought she heard the music begin again, at the edge of her perception. However, now she was ready. She took up the yoga stance she'd selected, closed her eyes, and addressed her own illness.

"I know you're not real," she said. "You're a false memory I created, something to punish myself with." She clasped in one hand the protective pentagram on her necklace, that she'd selected after much consideration, for its shape, feel, and materials. "I bring to the surface all the strength of the woman I am. I gather everything that can help me, I summon those forces to me. There is no such thing as an evil force that can harm me."

"Well, that's bollocks."

Autumn's eyes snapped open. She saw that a customer had entered somehow without ringing the bell, an angry-looking old lady it took a moment for her to recognise.

"Are you going to stand there spouting New Age wankery," said Judith, "or are you going to help me?"

———————

Judith was someone Autumn had heard about from her other customers ever since she'd opened the shop— someone who might have been in her core customer base, an actual local practitioner of . . . well, what Judith was actually into varied depending on who was telling the story. She had, it seemed, been thrown out of every local coven and circle from Swindon to Cirencester. "Aleister Crowley in a frock," as one white witch had put it, letting out a long sigh of recalled exasperation.

The fact that, despite that, Judith had never actually ventured into the magic shop had long been a source of nagging worry to Autumn. So her being here now was perhaps actually a positive sign, a synchronicity show-ing that the universe and Autumn's mind were now on the same upward path. Judith slapped a shopping list into her hand and marched round after her, grabbing each item off the shelves as Autumn found it. Judith seemed to share the occasional feeling that some of her customers expressed, that Witches was perhaps not arranged for browsing.

The old woman seemed to have an urgent desire to assemble a collection of items and ingredients that indi-cated a need on her part to shortly practice the craft in a rather worrying way. Autumn had tried and failed to communicate with her many other customers recently who'd also come here looking for troubling items, but this was different. Having Judith Mawson here was both a major coup and the chance to help an old lady who might be scared, lonely, confused even. "You seem," she said, as Judith threw another sprig of herbs into her bas-ket, "to be seeking protective ingredients, protective crystals. It's all about protection for you today."

Judith grunted.

"So is there some new situation in your life, some new problem which has made you seek such protection?"

Judith stopped, as if realising she wasn't going to get away without being talked at, and seemed to consider for a moment. "Nothing you can help with. I've found my materials in nature rather than in this jumble sale of a shop because you don't believe in magic. Now things have gotten to a bloody terrifying point where I need everything you've got as well as everything I've got. You're asking because you want to know if *you* need protection. The answer is yes, girl, loads of it, right now."

Autumn found her nails had dug into the palms of her hands. She made herself breathe. "Whatever *seems* to be happening, with the proper mental adjustment—"

"You won't save yourself with frigging aromatherapy. You at least have the sense to be wearing that." She pointed at the pentagram around Autumn's throat. "The sealed nut can work wonders, with sacrifice and whatnot. What you do with that nugget of actual useful info is up to you." Judith opened her handbag and dumped everything from her shopping basket into it with one chuck, then reached in her pocket, immediately found the exact money needed, and slapped it into Autumn's palm. "Magic is real," she said. "Stop running away. You've had some contact with the fairies of the Summerland, whether you're aware of it or not. I can smell it on you. If they come back, now the borders are wobbly, don't accept any invitations or cheques. If they say they can take you to meet royalty, they don't mean at Buckingham Palace, and you're not prepared for what you'd see."

Autumn was too shocked by her words to speak, and before she could muster urgent questions, Judith was marching out. "I might have to come back," she called, "even at these prices."

Autumn was about to follow, but then she heard once more, distantly, from behind the shop, the music. She'd just been told everything she'd fended off was true. It was like the sound was laughing at her.

———————

That morning, Lizzie had found Mr. Parks asleep in his nursing home, his breathing shallow, his son and daughter taking turns at his bedside. She had taken the opportunity, when his consciousness had surfaced briefly and he'd greeted her, to pray with him and administer the last rites. She'd done all this, not feeling the words herself. She'd been there as he'd passed away, holding his hand. Then she'd gone to the church, looked again at the wad of cash on the collection plate, and still not been able to touch it. She'd finally grabbed the plate, and hidden it under a duster inside the organ stool. She'd gone home to the vicarage and found she was too tired to make tea. She'd slumped onto the sofa, and soon she was asleep.

In her dream, Joe walked beside her again, on the road where she'd killed him. "Take the bloody money," he said, "give it to the poor. They don't care about what's going on inside your stupid head."

"I know," she said, luxuriating in being arm in arm with him, knowing it was all going to go wrong, but—in a dream—not knowing why or how.

"Maybe faith doesn't suit you anymore."

"This isn't actually you, is it?"

"Right. I'm just the sensible bit of you. I'm not 'watching over you from the other side.' There probably *isn't* an other side."

Lizzie's feelings on the afterlife had always been complicated. The Bible was actually much stronger on the idea that everyone was going to be resurrected together, physically, at what sounded like the end of the universe, than it was on the idea of heaven. "I never thought you were playing guitar with Jimi Hendrix."

"Do you want me to stop meeting you in dreams?"

She shoved him playfully. "Of course not!"

He staggered into the road just in time for the car to hit him again.

Lizzie woke slowly, every muscle aching. She felt too lost in grief to cry. One year gone, and she still felt like this. One year was how long people thought you were allowed to grieve. Maybe something had to give. Maybe that thing was her. The money was just money. She would write and post her resignation letter to the bishop, then go and get the money and pay it directly into the food bank charity's account, and then she would go far away. That row of decisions, falling silently in her head like demolished tower blocks, made her feel the closest to contentment she had in weeks. She hauled herself to her feet, and stumbled towards the first of them.

———————

Autumn stood by the counter, shaking, listening to the increasing volume of the music outside. Judith had arrived in her shop, like something out of the writings of Jung, at the very moment Autumn had been calling in everything she could to help her. What she'd said had matched what was in Autumn's head. Everything in her rationalist readings of magic said she should listen to the words of the wise woman who'd stepped over her threshold.

She had to face the possibility that what had happened to her was true. It was that or collapse, break down, curl up into a ball.

She made her decision. She went to the aisle of unicorn ornaments and found the most pointy of them. She strode to the back door and flung it open. She marched out into the car park her shop shared with the hot stone massage place and the accountancy business. The music was clear out here, blaring, terrifying. Other shop owners must have heard it. If they had, though, why weren't they out here complaining? "Where are you, you bastard?" she yelled, aware that she was giving her neighbours plenty to talk about.

He walked out into the light.

She had to take a step back. She had no idea of what he'd walked out of, if there had been a shadow there or . . . but no, now she couldn't do anything but look at him.

He was real.

He was exactly the same as he'd been all those years ago: so achingly thin, like a skeleton in leather trousers— leather jacket, hair down his back, eyes that looked every moment like he was going to take some sort of immediate and drastic action. He was carrying a radio straight out of the 1950s. It was playing the music—the music that had suddenly become absolutely clear and played by instruments no human had ever played: utterly impossible in the way it was constructed and yet obviously natural and terrifying on that basis alone, as if the sound itself opened up possibilities beyond this world. Autumn felt dizzy. She was breathing too fast. Was she hallucinating?

He switched off the radio and she nearly fell with relief at the silence. He was looking at her. Like she was the object of his next immediate and drastic action. "Digital," he said, pointing to the radio. "Better than the old panpipes, eh?" His accent was, as always, impossible to place, an accent they didn't make anymore.

She could find no response.

"Can I come in?"

"No!" She hated even talking to him, that acknowledgement he was really here. She had her defences. She was not going to let them down by inviting him in.

"You're looking lovely today."

She was frozen with anger.

"I've been trying to make you come out and see me. I didn't think you were going to pay attention to my summons. I wondered if you'd forgotten the music."

"I tried to."

"What?" He looked startled. "Why?" He took a step closer, those eyes searching her face. She made herself stand her ground. "Oh. You thought I . . . wasn't real." She remembered how he could read things like that from faces. "You actually thought all the beauty I showed you, all the treasures I shared with you . . ."

He sounded like he was actually getting angry, like he was the injured party. That gave her the right sort of anger to allow her to speak. "All you took from me!"

"Took? That's damned ungracious. You held my hand willingly. You entered my nation willingly—"

"You shoved me in!"

"Well, okay, yes, but only because you were hesitating. And what did I say to you immediately afterwards?"

If this was all true, then she remembered that, and she didn't want to. "That's not the point."

He roared at her. "*What did I say?*"

She stumbled *backwards*, feeling the force of his voice in her head. She used everything she'd learned to put a boundary around who she was and shoved him back out again.

He leapt back, as if he'd been slapped. He stared at her, sizing her up once again. "Oh, you've been studying. Interesting *flavour* to it. Practical. Different. A bit . . ." he gestured to his radio, "modern, like."

She had actually faced him down. The relief and exultation inside her threatened to make her start laughing or sobbing, and if she started she felt like she might not stop. If these were memories, not dreams or imaginings, then she remembered what had happened and she had to keep the moral high ground. "You said that every step I took was of my own free will. But I don't know how much you were influencing me to stay."

"Not at all, because you actually bloody left in the end, didn't you? I told you what you had to do to go home—"

"To let go of you . . . of your hand . . . for more than a hundred heartbeats. That's also true. But again—"

"You put it to practical use. You tried it. It worked. You ran out on me." He stopped, suddenly realising. "Are you saying I forced myself on you, influenced you to—?"

"Did you?"

"No. Because I'm a prince of the blood, not some human cowson, out for whatever he can get in his short lifetime. As if I'd soil such honour for you." She swore at him. He looked pleasingly outraged. "I didn't even lie to you, did I?"

"You didn't tell me where we were going."

"You still don't believe it now, so you wouldn't have believed it then."

"I'm talking about informed consent here."

"You consented *after* you saw the Summerland. Several times."

"You kept me—"

"I did not keep you."

"I was in there, in the kingdom, for—"

"A weekend."

"A year! It was a weekend for us in there, but for me it was a year away from home! Thanks to you, I lost my job, my family thought I'd run away or been murdered—!"

He stared at her. She couldn't read his face. "I can navigate across the border, I could have brought you back to the right point, but you ran—"

She didn't want to hear it. "I got out of your bed,

I . . . I went for a walk, and I kept counting heartbeats."
She remembered . . . she had to accept that was the right
word now . . . she remembered her awe at the clusters
of what she now knew to be magic ingredients growing
all over the building, a tree or cave or something which
had seemed like part of the landscape, the bright fields
of what her reading had since told her were things of
value to her craft seen through circles and gaps, the sheer
meaning everywhere. She had thought since, on those
few occasions when she'd allowed herself to imagine the
experience to be real, that what they called magic in this
world was just a gathering of scraps from that one. Then,
however, came the part of the dream that hurt her. The
curiosity about how all the corridors and branches and
breezes led one way, to an enormous door that was open
just a crack. How she had run, knowing her time was
short, to that door, and had looked inside like a child
expecting to see a secret. She had seen . . . her memory
shied away from it still. "I saw . . . I saw your father, on
his throne. I saw . . . !" She didn't want to remember the
sight, slammed the door in her mind now.

"You saw what he 'really' looked like?"

"Yes!"

"What I must 'really' look like, whatever this *really*
word means?"

"Yes!"

"And you ran from the sight of my father, leaving him furious at such judgement of him on your part, offended to the depths of his pride, which is why he—who is, himself, the land and also thus the border—made you arrive back a little late. When he didn't have to let you go at all."

So . . . so that had been deliberate? She just shook her head. Couldn't deal. "You make it sound like I should be grateful."

"You ran away because you realised I wasn't so attractive without my makeup. Because I'm not a young white male."

Something felt sick inside her. She checked her own defences, found he wasn't trying them. "You're twisting my words. This is what you do, you trick people."

"People trick themselves and blame us. Whatever 'us' is the latest us."

"You . . . you can't be saying . . ." She needed to make clear to him the tremendous hurt he'd caused, what the shock of what she'd seen and the time away had done to her. She needed to tell him about the harm done by the stories she'd made up for herself and others about where she'd been in that missing year, stories that she'd come to half believe herself, about the distance the experience had put between her and her family, between her and Lizzie. She found she had no words to do that now, but she would have some one day. Now, though, there was something more urgent to ask. "Listen. Why have you come back? Why are you here?"

"Because trouble is coming. You can help."

"I'm not going to help you." She indicated the pentagram at her throat, remembering what Judith had said. "This protects me from going with you."

He looked hurt. "You'd need cold iron for that, I could walk through that thing. Not that I intend to. Not with me being so disgusting to you. And as for that—" He gestured vaguely towards the unicorn ornament she'd forgotten she was clutching, "it's only just occurred to me that it's meant to be a weapon and not a vastly inauthentic gift. Listen. My father—"

"I don't want to hear about your father!"

"My father is considering going to war. Those old fools at that town meeting last night, they don't know what they're up against. Only one of them seems prepared, and nobody was listening to her, so I came to you."

Autumn found herself wrong-footed. Again. "Your father is considering going to war against a supermarket?"

"You've all spent decades ignoring it, but the shape of this town, the magic you call 'planning permission,' it's vitally important. This town is the lynchpin that holds all the barriers in place."

"The barriers?"

"Like the one you stepped over."

"Was *pushed* over!"

"Don't start that again."

"If I could do that, how is it a barrier?"

"Well, obviously the barriers allow a certain amount of traffic, passage to those who know what they're doing, at the proper times and places. Did you ever go looking for that border again?"

"No."

"Oh, and I see that's actually true. Weird. If the barriers collapse completely, there'll be chaos, disaster, as everything from the other worlds tries to rush in and plunder at once. Rather than allow that, my father will intervene to establish order, with sword and spear and glamour. By 'glamour,' I don't mean he'll be—"

"I *know.*"

"To human beings it won't look or feel like a war, it'll be more like . . . one of those modernist paintings you lot do, if it melted. Inside all your brains. Forever. That's the message I came to deliver: you have to get your people to vote the right way or, failing that, find some other way to stop this happening. If you don't sort this, we will."

It boggled Autumn to think cosmic powers from other worlds paid more attention to local news than she did. "I can't deliver some mad message to the whole town. They won't . . . believe me." Again. He was trying to put her through her ordeal again.

He looked disappointed in her. "I don't mind if my father goes to war," he said. "I get to take heads. I haven't had that pleasure in a while. I came back here because I was worried about you. About all of you." He sighed. "Look at you. Shaking. Furious. But if I asked you to come with me—"

"No. I can resist you now."

"I said 'ask.' And I won't ask. But you would." He switched his radio back on, and Autumn flinched, but now instead of the unearthly sounds of his home, it was playing smooth jazz. "Nice," he said. "We don't have that at home." He took a sudden, deliberate stride and once again, without her seeing where he went, he was gone.

Autumn slumped against the wall, breathing hard. It was all true. It was all true, and she had completely failed to deal. She needed help. No. No. They *all* needed help. Who was going to believe her? Could she even make herself try to convince . . . ? No. It didn't matter what happened to her, for everyone's sake she had to try. First she had to find Judith and tell her they were now on the same side. Because they'd make a great PR team: the mad woman and the old lady everyone hated. But where else could she start? Clasping her unicorn ornament to her, she rushed back into the shop and locked the door behind her.

4

Judith ran a line of silver paint, with several of the ingredients she'd bought from the magic shop in it, around the edge of her window sill. This was the last one. It was getting dark outside. She'd spent a couple of hours covering every entrance to the house, making sure she at least had a redoubt, somewhere to run back to if things tonight went pear-shaped. She had been thinking about possible allies, and had realised there was only one possibility, and that was going to be a bloody awkward conversation, but if she was going to go on the attack, she needed all the help she could get. She looked up at the sound of a knock on the door.

"That'll be your boyfriend," Arthur called from upstairs.

"If only!" Judith yelled back. She went to open the door, checking as she did so that the line she'd painted around it earlier was still intact. She opened the door to find nobody there. A meaningful absence of person. A sharp smell made her sneeze, a different scent to that of the figure who'd come from the woods, but just as troubling. She saw what she was smelling: in the middle of her front door had been painted, in red, the three lines of a downwards-facing triangle. She realised immediately what the shape signified. All you needed were white letters in a reassuring font across it and you had the Sovo brand logo. She grabbed her coat, called out to Arthur that she was just popping out for five minutes, and was out the door before he could say anything scathing in reply.

———————

Autumn had marched around the town in the late afternoon dark, trying to find Judith, having realised that she had no idea where she lived. She'd hoped to find someone who knew her. She was about to look in on the Plough and ask Terry, who worked behind the bar there, when she saw, across the Market Place, Lizzie. She was standing beside the post box under the streetlight, a letter in her hand, and visibly hesitating. She was crying. Perhaps yesterday—earlier that day even—Autumn would have made sure Lizzie didn't see her and gone on her way. Now, feeling as vulnerable as she did, she didn't seem to have room for resentment. She knew now that the impossible things she'd studied were real. It didn't matter what Lizzie thought was true. As Lizzie seemed to be making herself raise the letter towards the slit in the box, Autumn found herself running across to her. "Hey," she shouted, "Lizzie, wait!"

Lizzie turned, startled. "I was just going to post this letter," she said, quickly wiping her eyes.

"Well . . . don't!"

"You don't even know what it is."

"No," and as she said it, Autumn found huge relief in still understanding her old friend, "but I know you don't want to post it."

————————

Lizzie let herself be led into the Plough. They found the snug was empty and they could talk in private there, the only sound being the quiz machine. Autumn got them two pints of Arkell's 3B, the first sip of which was very welcome. "A lot's happened to me today," she said, sitting down facing Lizzie.

Lizzie found herself actually laughing. That Autumn could have dragged her in here having found her in that state and then led with what *she'd* been doing . . . that was very her. Very her was good right now. "Me too," she said, "I've come to a big decision I'm sure will please you—"

"No, listen. This is what I wanted to tell you before, only . . . has anything impossible ever happened to you?"

Lizzie had to take another drink and consider this change of pace for a moment. "I suppose the moments when I've . . . *thought* . . . I was having some sort of communication with God—"

Autumn waved aside the religious stuff. "I mean something that made you feel bad?"

Lizzie opened her mouth in exasperation at having her subtext run over yet again. Then she closed it again as she realised there *was* something. "Once I'd posted my *letter*—" Autumn gestured at her to get past that. "I was about to go back to the church and try to force myself to touch a large sum of money given to me as a donation for the poor."

Autumn's eyes narrowed, as if this wasn't quite what she was after, but she was too interested to let it go. "Why can't you?"

"I don't know. I've started to feel . . . that perhaps the world is just . . . chairs and tables and physical objects and that's all."

Again, Autumn didn't follow through on the implications of that. "So that means it's just money."

"Yes. I know. That's what I don't get about my own brain. Well done on putting your finger on that. Cheers." Lizzie took another deep gulp of her pint.

"Listen, this psychologist once asked a group of people if they'd sit in a chair that had belonged to a serial killer, that had been in his house—"

Lizzie shook her head. "No."

"Why?"

"I'd want it cleaned."

"It's been cleaned."

"Steam cleaned?"

"It's clean, okay?"

"Still, no."

"Because?"

"Because: euw."

"And almost everyone says that. When it's just a chair. I think that reaction is hardwired into peoples' brains, like they *know* there's something more to the world. I used to think that was just a sign that symbols were important."

Lizzie found herself astonished. "'Used to?' I thought you didn't believe in—?"

"That's the impossible thing that's happened to me today. Okay, listen . . ." Autumn started to tell her story, and Lizzie found she was going to need another pint.

————————

Judith strode quickly through the twilight streets of Lychford, seeing the Sovo symbol painted, at uneven intervals, on roughly half the doors. One of the marked doors opened as Judith approached, and she realised the figure emerging was someone she vaguely new from the quiz nights, a woman called . . . was it Lydia something? In Judith's head she was labelled as "annoying woman who talks only about false teeth."

"Have you seen the state of your door?" Judith called.

"What?" said Lydia, turning to look. "Paint's peeling a bit . . ."

Judith realised she couldn't see the mark. "You're against Sovo, aren't you?"

Lydia confirmed that she was. Before she could ask any questions or find a way to mention her dentures, Judith continued on her way, matching marks on doors to "Stop the Superstore" posters in the windows. These were surely the addresses of everyone planning to vote against. She turned into Ford Street, heading south out of the Market Place, and stopped, then stepped back into the shadows when she saw what was up ahead.

A young woman in a business suit, who Judith vaguely remembered from the meeting, had a paint pot in her hand, and was checking something, presumably addresses, on her phone. She confirmed her latest target, then walked up to the door and marked it with a well-practiced three slashes. Judith wondered if anyone else but her could see this job being carried out. Then she became aware that she was not alone, that someone stood at the corner with her. She didn't give the new presence the satisfaction of a reaction. "What are you really?" she asked.

David Cummings stepped from the shadows. "I've been very clear about my job title."

She couldn't see anything extraordinary about this man, any more than she had when he'd been on stage at the meeting, but, ah, there, now he wasn't concealing how big he really was. She could suddenly feel the gravity of him. He was holding himself back, even, letting only a little of himself extrude into the world. His true scale would cause panic in the streets. Judith had only twice in the past been anywhere near one of the great powers. She now had a primal urge to get down on her knees and beg for mercy. Well, sod that. "So it's not just foolishness on your part. You're doing this deliberately. Is Sovo some sort of front for—?"

"We're exactly who we say we are, doing exactly what we've told everyone we're planning to do."

"Apart from the bit about painting on opponents' doors."

He chuckled, entertained by her. "If they can't see it, what's the difference?"

"What are the symbols on the doors for?"

"You know, I've got tons of money to throw around. How would you fancy a Saga tour of the Caribbean for yourself and a friend, whoever that might be? Chance to get away? Start a new life? Before it's too late?"

She was pleased that he hadn't felt able to tell her what the symbols were for. "It would be too late, though. The world would have a bloody hole in it. Why do you *want* the barriers around the town to fall?"

"There's a word people in business use a lot: *disruptive*. The market can never be stable, the best it can be is falling apart in useful ways. Like the universe in general, really. To disrupt the market in your favour is now seen as being the ultimate achievement. Create a climate of absolute uncertainty, continual fear about enormous change, and you'll see people's . . . well, I was about to say 'true selves,' but they don't really have true selves, they're continually falling apart too . . . you'll see people concentrate on looking after themselves and their own, grabbing for familiar symbols. The right . . . *brands*, shall we say, can prosper hugely then, in the ultimate disruption."

"Oh, you'd enjoy that."

He looked genuinely hurt. "I'm not sure *enjoy* is the right word. I'm just doing my job. Looking forward to some time off, honestly, after the end of the universe. Now, are you sure we can't interest you in coming onside?"

Judith knew he could kill her with a glance. He was limited, though, by the role he'd taken on, by the rules of the game he'd decided to take part in. "Sorry, love," she said. "I'm too old for shop work." She marched off before he could tempt her with anything else. She didn't want him to see how much he'd scared her. She had to find her only ally, but before that, she had to have a go at getting rid of that symbol on her door.

———————

"After I came back to the . . . the real world," Autumn was saying to Lizzie, "I was in a psychiatric hospital for a while. I made the mistake of trying to tell people about the impossible beings I'd met."

"That's why you never got back in touch," whispered Lizzie. She didn't know what to make of what she was hearing. It was clear that, from what Autumn had told her about her "visit" from some sort of supernatural being today, and the dire, if vague, warning he'd delivered, her friend now believed utterly in the story she'd just told about where she'd been all that time. Was the bit about the psychiatric hospital the only thing that was true? Were their roles now going to be reversed, with Autumn the believer and her the sceptic? Her training had given her insight into how to deal with mental illness, but she didn't like the idea of having to apply that training to Autumn.

Autumn smiled the wry and somewhat bitter smile that Lizzie had seen when she'd come to see her, earlier—when she'd failed, she realised, to tell her about all this. "When you told people about the impossible beings *you'd* met, they gave you a job."

"Is this why you didn't want to step inside my church? Oh. You're not going to tell me you've become a..." She'd started to say the word and realised she had to finish, making sure she did so with every ounce of her attentiveness and positivity. "A vampire?"

"What? Of course not!"

"Of course not. Right."

"You're the one who thinks wine turns into blood!"

"Well, I don't, didn't, actually, in my brand of... and *now*—"

"It's just there's something about your church. When I walked up to that threshold, I... felt something. In those moments when I let myself believe in it, I've sometimes felt my time in that other world changed me, *tainted* me—"

"Oh no, oh no, that's so the opposite of what we... I... stood... stand for. You felt welcome when you stepped in, didn't you? Please tell me you did."

"I felt... like that building is... connected to something, and I can feel it. I sometimes feel it at other places in Lychford."

Lizzie blew out a long breath. She didn't know what to believe. "Perhaps I should show you this money."

"Was it maybe something to do with Cummings himself?"

"Well, he is a being of tremendous power and evil," said Judith, sitting down beside Lizzie and placing her pint on the table in one movement. "You get on your way, shopkeeper, I need to talk to the grown-up." By which she meant Lizzie.

"Sorry," said Lizzie, "we're in the middle of—"

"No time for that. My name, Reverend, is Judith Mawson. Did your predecessor tell you much about this town? Did he mention my name?"

"No." Lizzie had heard of the old woman, from a number of terrified parishioners. She was, she assumed, someone whom Autumn would have had as a customer, but the look on her friend's face was desperate, thankful.

"Listen," said Autumn, "I've been trying to find you—"

"You're talking over her thinking more seriously about my question."

Actually, Lizzie *was* thinking about it. Her predecessor, Frank, had left a very terse note, giving her the bare minimum of information. She'd asked the churchwardens about everything from the organist to the accounts, until she was sure no surprises awaited her. They had always had, though, she realised, a look on their faces as if they were waiting for someone else to tell her something awkward. "No, but—"

"I know it's all true," said Autumn. "A prince of the blood came to warn me. He says something terrible is going to happen."

Judith looked to Autumn with new interest. Lizzie was sure she was about to see the start of a beautiful *folie à deux*, and she wasn't sure she wanted that inflicted on her friend. "I'm afraid I'll have to insist—"

"Sorry about this," said Judith, "but we need to get past all that time-wasting incredulity." She grabbed Lizzie's nose between her fingers and viciously twisted before letting go. Lizzie yelled, blinded by tears of pain, furious.

Judith was looking at the blood on her fingers. She put them in her mouth, tasting it. "You never thought," she said, as if reading from a book she didn't understand, "that Joe was playing guitar with Jimi Hendrix."

Lizzie found the anger draining from her, replaced by sheer vertigo and rising fear. She looked to Autumn, who nodded, willing her to believe it. Lizzie found blood was running from her nose and fumbled for a tissue.

"No floundering," said Judith, "no arguing. Good. That's how a vicar of Lychford should be. Some of your predecessors found a packet of Oat So Simple an intellectual challenge. Now, come on, you too I suppose." She nodded a little reluctantly to Autumn. "It's time you knew everything." She threw back her pint in one long swallow, slammed it back onto the table, got up and headed out of the pub without looking over her shoulder.

"I'm going with her," said Autumn. "Lizzie, I have to know."

"Yeb," said Lizzie through the tissue. "I hab do doo."

Judith led them through the darkness to the church, which surprised Lizzie, because she couldn't imagine being taught anything about a space she'd already explored. On the way, she listened to Autumn's story, asking at intervals for more detail. Autumn only hesitated at the threshold of the building for a moment this time. Lizzie switched on the lights and Judith took them over to one of the enormous displays of blooms that the flower ladies provided to decorate the nave. "I should have come to see you when you first got here. I'd sort of guessed Frank hadn't done his duty in explaining the extra responsibilities of someone officiating here. It didn't seem urgent."

"You could have pinched her nose," said Autumn. "How does that work, anyway? Is there information in the blood, in the DNA maybe—?"

Judith stopped and visibly winced. "'DNA' my arse. If you're coming along, I don't want you coming out with bloody science all the time. You'll be looking at everything through the smallest window."

"The smallest window," said Autumn, "might have the clearest glass."

"It doesn't. It's muddy."

"But the other windows will stay as they are, but this window could be replaced by . . . a big set of French windows, when science catches up with magic."

Judith rolled her eyes. "I'm trying to show you the ineffable and you're planning an extension."

"Ibe reddy do libben," Lizzie said through her hanky.

"The flower ladies," said Judith, turning back to the display, "keep these refreshed for a reason, which they probably think these days is just about good taste." She picked up the enormous vase and hauled it aside.

Behind the flowers, Lizzie was surprised to see revealed a painting, faded colours on a surviving remnant of the original plasterwork of the church, part of what, for most of the building's life, would have been a vibrant background of many hues. The painting was a map of the town. It looked ancient.

Around the central crossroads of buildings were family names of outlying farms, some of which were still familiar. There was the church itself, there was the forest and the river.

Outside all of that, however, were rough borders in different colours that didn't correspond to anything Lizzie knew about the shapes of parishes or counties. Inside those areas were painted what looked like demons, strange dancing humanlike figures, even chaotic swirls, like storms. "This map of Lychford," said Judith, "dates back to when the church was built, in Saxon times, replacing a stone circle, which replaced a longbarrow, the remains of which are under the crypt." Lizzie knew of no records of such a barrow. "Here"—Judith pointed to the outlying features of the map—"are what borders Lychford—other realms, of the foul and the fair, the horrible and the wonderful, and some stuff beyond understanding." She said that as if it were a phrase that had been repeated to her. "You won't find these on a sat nav."

Lizzie looked to Autumn. She was staring at the map, her expression half relieved, half horrified. She had a hand on the end of a pew, as if she continually had to reassure herself of reality. Lizzie took that hand in hers.

"As the town grew around the river crossing," continued Judith, "and became a point where the farmers could sell their produce, locals who knew the craft realised that by building here they were upsetting a delicate balance that had been sorted out long before people came to

Britain. That balance protected a very rare, perhaps unique crossing place, from which all these different worlds could be reached. Perhaps the people back then were skilled enough to work that out themselves, perhaps they were visited and given some sort of ultimatum. At any rate, they planned the town with that balance in mind, worked out exactly where to build, using the shape of what they made to seal off the borders and prevent any accidental blundering about. The church, when the Saxon shire reeve decided one was needed, was designed as a major part of that effort. You could say it's one of the pins that keeps things fastened."

"That's what I can feel," said Autumn.

"Ah, something rubbed off on you in fairyland. As well as the other way round."

Autumn stepped forward, and pointed at the place on the map with the dancing figures. "*That's* where I went. That's . . ." She peered closer at one of the figures. "Oh my God. That's him. That's Finn."

Judith tutted. "And after meeting him, she still didn't believe! Is it really that hard to pay attention to what's shagging you?"

Autumn looked back to her, furious. "I could have used this bloody map a few years back. I could have used your help when I got home."

Judith's expression remained absolutely fixed—

something that meant, Lizzie knew from dealing with many ladies of the older generation, that big emotions were moving underneath. "If I'd known," she said, "I'd have come to see you." She looked back to Lizzie before she was forced to register any further emotion from Autumn. "Because the church is part of the defences, the vicar and the others who know the secrets have always worked together."

"De ubbers?" asked Lizzie.

"Well..." Judith looked suddenly troubled. "Your churchwardens must know what the last vicar's traditionally meant to have told you, but if they believed it they'd have made sure. So, since old Mrs. Hitchmough moved to Bournemouth I suppose it's just me. I'm not the most sociable person. I've got issues I don't talk about and others wouldn't want to hear. Which, when summat terrible's about to happen, is just my bloody luck."

"Dabid Cubbings," said Lizzie, "he said—"

Judith grabbed her nose again and just as Lizzie was about to yell from the pain again, she realised that the pain had actually stopped and that her nose had stopped bleeding. She lowered her handkerchief. "He talked about changing the shape of the church."

"Makes sense."

"You said he was a being of tremendous power and evil, but I've looked him up. He's got a wife and family.

He's on LinkedIn."

"Those are the worst sort. He's had himself incarnated. His wife and family probably aren't aware of what he is."

"Which is?"

"There are lots of names, none of them pleasant, some of which could lead you astray." She marched towards the door. "You'll learn a lot more where we're going."

———————

As Judith led them down to the river walk, then under the bridge, picking her way with more enthusiasm than skill along the narrow path in the freezing dark, Autumn started to feel more and more afraid. Suddenly, without even a torch to help her, Judith veered off into the darkness of the forest. She immediately fell over a branch, but was pushing herself up using her stick before Lizzie or Autumn could reach her. "This path should be safe," she said. "It's changed, but only a bit. I still know it."

"Is there some rule," said Lizzie, her breath billowing in the air, "against using a torch?"

"Of course not. I just . . . thought I could do without." She allowed Lizzie to find an app that made the screen of her iPhone light up, and, having been shown how to hold it, kept going, keeping Lizzie and Autumn close enough to catch her if she fell.

"I haven't been out here much," said Autumn, "not since . . . you know—"

"Since you became a Fairy Wife. As they call it."

"—but this footpath only goes to Borton."

"If you walk it the usual way, it does. Look." Autumn followed her pointing stick and saw, in the light of the moon that was now rising over the hill, that a crossing with a wooden signpost lay ahead. She felt nauseated to see it.

"That's . . . not usually there," said Lizzie. She went up to the sign and touched it, like it was something out of Narnia. Autumn hated seeing that reaction. That was what she'd felt on the way in, too. One of the direction indicators on the old sign said "Borton," pointing in front of them. The other, going off at an angle, was blank. Or was it? Autumn felt she could see something there, but it was like when you looked at the stars and saw the fainter objects only out of the sides of your eyes. When you looked directly, they vanished again, and so did this.

She saw Judith looking appraisingly at her. "I can't see it," she said.

"At least," Judith said, "you know summat's there. There are three ways to walk the old paths. One is by sacrifice." She pulled a pin from her hair, and struck it across her own thumb like striking a match, a worryingly practiced gesture that produced a flick of blood. She squeezed her hand into a fist, then put the bloodied palm flat on the pathway that led off at an angle. "Or there's an appeal to a higher power," she nodded to Lizzie. "What you do. Or you can use what's already there, manipulate it, like judo or summat. I've heard that if you live where there are lots of people there are other options too, but that's all for a hedge witch like me."

Autumn couldn't help herself. This stuff was like a lifeline for her rationality to cling to. She was, she realised, going to have to keep using logic to deal with it, as she always had before, or she'd be lost. "That's all really interesting. If there are rules, then didn't you ever want to work out *why* there are rules, how it all connects—"

"To science? That was going to set us all free, but here we are, free to buy the latest gadget, free to be watched on CCTV and Google Whatever It Is." Judith was suddenly in Autumn's face, animated by an anger Autumn hadn't seen in her before. "This stays secret, for the people who don't have much, who live in the gaps, who have to find some way to get by. If you start blabbing about what I show you today—"

"No, no," Autumn held up hands, not wanting to hear whatever threat Judith was about to come out with. She'd already spent so much of her life being scared by magic, she hated that the old woman was scaring her too. "Out of respect to you, okay? I will deal with this my own way, but I won't go calling up the *Sun* and trying to get them to believe it. As if."

"You say," said Lizzie, who'd been following, looking fascinated, "that big companies shouldn't have this, but aren't Sovo a big company?"

"Sovo are just doing what they always do, unaware. Dave Cummings is riding them. You still don't really believe, do you?"

"It's . . . a lot to take in."

"Never mind, our next stop will sort that out." She led them round two turns through the trees, and stopped at the edge of a clearing. She struggled to switch off the iPhone light until Lizzie showed her how to do it, then as their eyes adjusted to the dark, she pointed. "There."

In the clearing stood a well. It looked simple, ancient. Autumn felt a great weight to it, like she had at the threshold to the church. There was no winch, but on the ground sat a metal bucket with a rope. "This is where," said Judith, "I lost my innocence. I was shown this by my mates, the older girls who played in the forest and had come to see the ways. Over the years they've all gone. Stupid old woman, never passing it along like I should have done. If I'd had a daughter—" She stopped, shook her head. "My mother knew, and she tried to stop me learning. She was scared, poor soul. My friends brought me here one summer night, and I wish it was summer now, but those that have no choice have to make do."

She went to pick up the bucket and threw it into the well, letting the rope trail behind it. It turned out there was a lot of rope in that coil. It kept going as Autumn looked incredulously at Lizzie. Finally, there was a distant splash. Judith began to haul it back up again. "This," she said, "will let you see things like I do. I had an inkling of it, like Autumn does, but this opened my eyes." She brought the bucket to the lip of the well. "Right then. Clothes off."

"What?" said Lizzie.

"No," Autumn shook her head.

"I'm really not up for—"

"It's bloody freezing!"

Judith sighed. "All right, all right. This water is from the river that runs between the worlds. It lets you see the truth. Is that what you want?"

"Yes," said Autumn.

"I want," said Lizzie, "to understand what's going on. So, okay, do you want us to drink it, or—?"

Judith threw the bucket of water over them.

Autumn shrieked at the shock of the impact. The cold went right through her coat, into her clothing. She was about to yell like Lizzie was doing when all of a sudden . . . it was like a curtain had fallen away from her vision. What had been a bare old stone well was now shining with symbols in golden inlay. The forest, stark and leafless, pulsated with the deep, hidden warmth of every tree. The moon was enormous, full of detail that was so fascinating it felt like it threatened to draw her up into it. The stars beyond it had infinite complexity, each with an individual life. Autumn had taken her fair share of illegal substances, back in the day. This was different to all of them. This was the drug that was everyday vision being cleansed from her body. This was what where Finn had taken her had been like, and with that thought didn't come fear, but enormous relief. The strange water in her clothes had become not a horrible burden but warming. She could feel it not evaporating, exactly, but sinking into her skin, becoming part of her, vanishing from the cloth as it sought out her flesh.

"That's why I said take your clothes off," said Judith. "For the next twelve months or so you'll see like I do. Then, if you want to, you can come back for another dose. Assuming any of us are still here."

"It's real, Lizzie," whispered Autumn.

Judith laughed at their expressions. "Just like my first time," she said. "Only without the lesbianism. Probably no time for that now."

"No," agreed Autumn, alarmed.

"Right," nodded Lizzie quickly, then seemed to feel

compelled to add, "not that there's anything wrong with that."

"You don't have to, I found out, afterwards," said Judith. "But they didn't tell me at the time. It was the sixties."

Lizzie looked like she'd suddenly realised something that troubled and excited her at the same time. "If I can see this . . ." She came to a decision. "I'm sorry," she said, and she turned and ran back down the path.

"Lizzie!" Autumn shouted after her.

"It's all right," said Judith. "I know where she's going."

5

They found Lizzie in her church, walking back and forth, desperately looking around. She turned to look at them almost accusingly. "Nothing." She took them over to the organ stool and opened it, and Autumn was startled to see just how much money she'd been talking about. She'd found that the miraculous detail and sense of hidden wonders had faded a lot when they'd returned to the normal path and especially in the town, but she'd still felt a sense of additional meaning and gravity at certain places, this church included. There was no divine presence here, though, not that she could feel, and the money was just money.

Judith put a hand on Lizzie's shoulder. "The higher powers choose when to show themselves."

"If you worked with my predecessor—"

"I don't know whether or not what you believe in is true, love. All I know is, it's your job to help protect the people in this town. "

Autumn watched Lizzie take a deep breath, then nod. "What do you want us to do?"

———————

Lizzie tried to keep a calm expression on her face as Judith led them into town. She wanted to jump every time she felt the presence of an underground river or saw some extra dimension to someone's expression as they trudged past. It would take some getting used to. The trouble was, as Judith had realised, it hadn't dealt with the enormous holes at the centre of her life. Indeed, it had emphasised them. "Can we see . . . dead people?" she asked. Which got a puzzled look from Autumn.

Judith took a moment to answer. "Sometimes," she said carefully. "But now I need you to see this." On random doors down the street, red symbols were shining. The symbols . . . it was like they stank. They had the same feeling about them that made you recoil from something that had been in your fridge too long.

Judith told them about her encounter with Cummings, and Lizzie felt glad she could at last bring something useful to the table. "It's like the Passover," she said, "the story in the Old Testament. The Angel of Death kills the firstborn of everyone who hasn't obeyed God's instructions to put a marking in sheep's blood on their door."

"God wanted that?" said Autumn.

"Yeah. He's changed a lot. But this is the other way round, right? It's a threat to the people *with* markings, if these are the ones who are against Sovo. It's a reversal, like an upside-down cross."

They went up to one of the houses that didn't seem to have anyone home. Lizzie was acutely aware that here she was, in her clerical collar, in which she didn't even allow herself to have more than a couple of pints, standing with two well-known local "characters," staring at people's doors. She could feel, actually literally now, the curtains twitching. The paint on the door felt warm to their faces. None of them wanted to touch it. "What if we got rid of the marks?" asked Autumn.

"Oh," Judith said brightly, "I hadn't thought of that."

"Sarcasm," said Lizzie, "about what is and isn't possible: not allowed now."

"I scrubbed my door," said Judith, "with every magical cleansing agent I could think of. *And* Cillit Bang! I just ended up burning my Brillo pads."

"I guess just painting over it—?" began Lizzie. Judith was silent. "Aha!" said Lizzie.

"You said sarcasm wasn't allowed," said Judith. "You two had better watch out about your own doors when you get home. Now we can see this stuff, we can be burned by it too. Sometimes ignorance is bliss."

Lizzie felt a little awkward. "I had to keep a bit above

it all, no sign for me."

"I, erm, was *for* the store . . . ," Autumn said. "It's not like they were going to sell magic stuff. Although maybe *now* . . ."

Lizzie decided there was something she could do. She looked around to make sure nobody was out on the dark street at this moment, then stepped up to the door. "In the name of the father—" She'd raised her hand to make the sign of the cross, but she found that she just couldn't complete it. What was this? Was some powerful force stopping her? No, just a feeling of . . . absurdity. Weakness. She *knew* it wouldn't work.

"This mark is made of actual paint," said Judith, gently, "no matter how weird and special that paint might be. If you could get a mark off a door by raising your finger—"

"That would be an actual miracle," said Lizzie. "I never was sure what I thought about those."

"We need to take a scientific approach," said Autumn. "No, wait, hear me out. You say it's actual paint. So let's try to find out more about it." She looked around, as if for inspiration, then found it. She pointed at the "Stop the Superstore" sign in the window of the house. "Can we get hold of one of those posters?"

———————

Jade Lucas felt she was doing okay, and with how things were at the moment, okay was better than okay. Okay meant she was just about up to the limit on her credit cards, but she paid the rent, and she wasn't in trouble with logbook or payday lenders like a lot of her mates. She'd been junior management at Sovo in Slough when Mr. Cummings had visited one lunchtime to give a pep talk. They'd all expected it to be the usual bollocks, but he'd been funny, and kind of harsh, and everyone agreed after that he'd been straight with them.

He'd talked about austerity not as something politicians talked about, something that'd be gone when the economy got better, but as a way to live your life. If you looked after number one, then you'd do better, and you'd be able to look after the people you loved. Jade didn't love anyone in particular, and he'd made her feel better about that, so she'd decided to take him up on one of his points about seizing every advantage. She'd walked beside him as he headed to his car and had said she'd do anything to get higher up in the company. He'd nodded, unsurprised, like this had happened before, and had asked her to get in with him, saying he'd clear it with her boss. In the back of his car, she'd been startled when he'd asked her to literally kiss his arse, but had hesitated only a moment before doing so, wondering how much further he'd want to go, and whether she'd really meant "anything." He'd been satisfied at that, however, and had offered her a contract, which she'd signed immediately.

She'd been moved, at the company's expense, to a nice new house near a local hub in Swindon, where she'd become part of an unusual sales strike force. They were called upon to do the weirdest things, most of which turned out to be a laugh, like today, where they'd been drawing the company logo on people's doors. Alec, her immediate boss, had said nobody would mind or notice, and they hadn't. Jade felt she'd learned a lot about human nature since joining the strike force. Now she was doing one last sweep before they all went back to the hotel, then off to a club in Gloucester, where hopefully there'd be some snort to be had, because she was knackered.

She'd finished her list, and she'd been told to also look out for houses not on it which now displayed anti-Sovo posters, the floating voters. There was one now, to her annoyance, in the window of . . . a shop that sold magic things. Used to the idea that nobody would object, Jade opened her pot of paint that smelled like the most gorgeous coffee, dipped in her brush, and made to mark the door.

Which was when some black girl in an amazing dress

and a bomber jacket opened the door and grabbed the pot and brush. "Not today, thank you," she said, and before Jade could react, her tools had been snatched inside and the door slammed in her face. Jade hammered on it, horrified at the thought of what might happen to her if she had to go back and tell Alec she'd lost her tools.

"Any trouble here, ma'am?"

She turned to see a policeman looking at her, a wry look on his face. She considered for a second saying she'd had some things stolen, but then she'd have to explain what she'd been doing. Alec didn't have to know. They just threw the stuff into a bin bag anyway, to be taken back to central office. Not telling him: that was looking after number one. "No trouble," she said, and headed off, wanting to put distance between her and that shop, and looking forward to her night out.

———————

Lizzie was looking around at a workshop full of bubbling test tubes and beakers with things dripping into them. There were what looked like ancient diagrams Blu-Tacked to the walls, but the back room of Autumn's shop looked more like a school science lab than a wizard's chamber. A moment ago, Autumn had returned triumphant, the pot of paint and brush in hand. They'd had to wait an hour, the lights on the shop front turned off, before someone had taken the bait. Lizzie applauded, and Judith nodded, one eyebrow raised, in appreciation.

"So," Lizzie went up to her, gesturing to the equipment, "this is where the magic happens."

"How long have you been waiting to say that?"

"Since you told me you owned the shop. But, you know: trauma."

"I had the workshop set up in my old house before I had the shop. I like making my own potions."

"It's all too scientific," said Judith.

"What do you use? A cauldron?"

"Obviously."

Lizzie picked up the brush, sniffing the red goo. The pungent smell made her cough. "We need to do some sort of chemical analysis," she said, "find out what's in this stuff. I can't . . . see . . . anything weird, not with my new senses, I mean."

"It's mostly red paint," said Autumn, "with a few herbs I stock in the shop."

Lizzie was impressed. "How did you work that out so quickly?"

Autumn held up the tin and pointed. "List of ingredients."

Lizzie saw she was right. "Wow. The powers of evil are kind of thorough."

"And it turns out, according to this, that the same herbs which went into my invisibility potion really can make something invisible."

"With the proper incantations and sacrifice during mixing," said Judith, "and the force of belief, which you wouldn't have been able to add."

"You sold an invisibility potion?" asked Lizzie.

"It was designed to provide solace, comfort, a sense of getting away from it all . . ."

"But not *invisibility*," said Judith.

"There was a disclaimer on the bottle," said Autumn. "Can we get on?"

Judith picked up a piece of paper and began to draw. "If what's in this stuff is just to make it invisible, then there has to be summat else going on to add other effects, like harming anyone who's got it on their door. Sacrifice and incantation will have gone into setting that up. The shape of the symbol might be important." She held up a drawing of the Sovo logo. "It has an unsettling aspect."

"Meaning—?" asked Lizzie.

"That's the sort of thing I say when I have no idea what I'm going on about."

"We can't get rid of the marks," began Lizzie.

"And painting over them won't make any difference," said Judith.

"And if this isn't about the paint, no amount of analysis can help us," said Autumn.

"We've got three days until the meeting," said Lizzie. "Sovo seem to be going to do something terrible to those planning on voting against, or maybe just stop them leaving their houses. If Dave Cummings gets his way and the new store gets built, it sounds like it might literally be the end of the world. So . . . what can we do?"

They looked at each other. None of them had an answer.

———————

The following evening, Shaun Mawson decided he'd go to sample one of Sunil Mehra's excellent chicken dansaks, and also perhaps two or three Cobra beers, rude not to, and at the same time, have a chat with the proprietor. So they found a table, and Shaun, while liberally distributing lime pickle on his papadum, made his position clear. "Okay, so she might be mad as toast, she believes a lot of weird stuff, her cooking's terrible, and she wears the same cardigans for weeks, until they smell like diesel, for some reason—"

"You're talking to me about your mother? Oh, dear." Sunil raised a hand to his waiter. "Keep the Cobra coming for PC Mawson."

"I'm here to say I think Mum *needs* something more

in her life. Even more so at the moment. I'm here to say . . . don't get discouraged. Okay?"

Sunil looked as if he was having trouble formulating a response, but before he could, someone else arrived at the table. It was Maureen, the mayor. Shaun had noted her on the way in, eating on her own, looking like she hadn't slept in days. She'd barely acknowledged his greeting. These days, every such hello must for her be either a gesture of support or the start of a row. "Excuse me," she said, "I couldn't help overhearing. This is difficult—"

Sunil had a chair brought over. "Please," he said, "it's everyone's night for difficult conversations. If you'd like me to leave you two to talk . . . I'd be delighted."

"No, because, well, I gather you and Judith are great friends, Mr. Mehra, and like Shaun I'm glad to see that. I just wanted to ask . . . oh dear, I shouldn't—"

Shaun had heard what everyone else in town had, that Maureen had taken money to support Sovo. He'd waited for anyone to allege it to him or to his superiors on an official basis, but the lack of such an approach had presumably meant that those opposed to the store had failed to find anything solid they could offer him. He'd always liked Maureen, because his mum had, to the tiny degree she liked anyone, but now he wasn't feeling especially gracious toward her. "If you've got something to say about Mum—"

"I saw her yesterday evening, going around town, looking at people's doors. Just going right up to them and staring at them. She was dragging the new vicar and that girl from the magic shop around with her, like she was trying to persuade them about something. I've seen her talking to someone who wasn't there—"

"I'm not sure I want to hear this." Mum hanging around with those two fitted in with her usual eccentricities, and when she'd called him about the magic shop the other day, there really had been someone trying to get in, though it had taken Shaun's eyes a moment to adjust to the gloom and see her, just like Mum had, oddly, said it would.

"No, please, I'm not saying she's like that all the time, I know she isn't, she's just . . . tough and a bit eccentric, and I like that. I just think . . . it's getting to all of us. So many people in this town are breaking under the strain, and I . . . I don't know what to do. What I'm saying is, she needs someone to talk to right now, and the way she looked at me the other day I know I can't . . ." She trailed off, then closed her eyes, as if trying not to cry, then had to quickly get up. "Excuse me," she said. "I've left some money." Then she was off and out the door.

Shaun looked carefully back to Sunil. "Now, that made what's happening with Mum sound a bit more serious than it is . . ."

Sunil sighed. "How long have I known your mother? Business as usual, by the sound of it."

Shaun made himself smile, but he wondered—given what he'd seen in the town just lately, with rows breaking out in the queue for the post office, people getting hate mail, postings on the town's website forum that had for the first time made the webmistress decide on a moderation policy—if whichever way the vote went, any of them could look forward to business as usual.

Lizzie took time, in the days before the meeting, to go and see her parishioners, particularly those she knew had symbols painted on their doors. What she most heard was a formless anger about how things were changing so fast, how someone had to stand up to the big companies who thought they ran everything. With her collar on, Lizzie still didn't feel able to agree out loud.

Those she talked to who wanted the store to come here had hardly embraced evil. They talked about how hard things were, how they needed to shop more cheaply without spending a lot of money on petrol, how they and their relatives needed the jobs Sovo would provide. There was something of a class divide there. Those who weren't well off tended to back the store on the basis of economic survival.

As Lizzie had seen so many times with victims, the harder your life had been, the harder it was to give yourself room for ethical choices.

So were born cycles of abuse.

Both sides had friends across the divide, people they were having trouble talking to. Lizzie went door to door, causing many raised eyebrows about her sudden presence on the doorsteps of especially the elderly. Everywhere she went, she asked people to keep talking to her.

She saw occasional wonders, with her new senses, in peoples' homes: animated love of beloved teddy bears, figures of departed loved ones with stony or caring faces. Those had scared her, though she hadn't shown it. She'd gone back to the vicarage, after leaving Autumn's workshop, wondering if she'd see Joe there, almost hoping. He hadn't been there. Something had changed, though: she now had a Sovo symbol on her front door.

They listened closely, and they worked fast.

She kept in touch with Autumn and Judith, heard they were both researching, trying to discover what exactly Sovo was attempting to do. All Lizzie could think of was how useless research would have been in the week before Passover. All she herself could do was attempt to pray, and she found she still didn't have it in her to do that. She wanted to go and take the money that still sat untouched in the collection plate and give it to the poor. She still couldn't, though Joe, in her dreams, was now yelling at her that she should.

"Are you my conscience now, my whole religion?" she angrily asked the memory of Joe, when she woke on the day of the council meeting and the deciding vote. "Is a single push of my hands why I do things now?"

Perhaps she hoped that the catastrophe to come, or preventing it, would confirm her faith, though she knew that was a selfish thought. The letter to the bishop remained unsent, but still sat in the out tray on her desk.

———————

Judith was getting increasingly desperate. She found the strain of it getting to her old body, making her shoulders ache, making her want to weep. The combination of incantation, purpose, shape, and whatever sacrifices had gone into the symbols on the doors was a code she couldn't crack. Nor could she think of anything which might get, for example, everyone who was for Sovo to leave town before the vote. It would take power beyond hers, and what little the novices could add, to get people to act against their own fervent wishes.

Sovo seemed to be doing only one thing, hinging everything on the mundane matter of tonight's vote, and presumably trying to influence it, exactly the sort of drama one expected from the major powers.

She had extended, through potion and ritual, all her senses, and found nothing sinister about the company or their representatives, apart from Cummings. So whatever they were doing depended on him. There were three approaches one could take: sacrifice, appeal to a higher power, or manipulation. She tried some experimental sacrifices: she pulled a tooth from her mouth and gave the pain to the forge of the fates. She prostrated herself before the aspects of the Goddess, before Lugus of the Skilful Hand, before, in final desperate gestures, T.S. Eliot and Ringo Starr. She could not think of any means to achieve manipulation.

She would pull some ancient thought out of her feeble excuse for a brain, then find it connected to nothing useful. She had made the mistake, for so many years, of keeping her knowledge in her head. So this morning she had decided she had almost certainly forgotten something important, and had gone up into her attic and found her old trunks containing the diaries she'd kept as a youth. She'd indexed them, she remembered. She was pretty sure that everything in the index had long ago become second nature to her. Certainly there was nothing under P for Protection that she didn't now do offhandedly, and nothing that could be applied to those doors to counteract whatever nastiness Sovo had planned for those inside. She ran her finger down the alphabet, and stopped at K.

K for Kill.

She found she was holding her breath. She flipped to the entry, and found something pressed between the pages. A twig. She'd remembered, she'd realised, somewhere at the back of her head. She'd tried to forget the boy, what he'd done to her. His name had been Robin. It was his fault . . . she didn't want to think about the curse he'd placed on her. She didn't need to. She lived with it every day. Robin had been from Lancaster, and he'd boasted of what he could do, and she'd been so bloody impressed, hadn't she? She'd gotten him to show her. They'd buried the squirrel together, buried it deep.

Could she do this? She had only this day left, and no other ideas. No time for second thoughts, no time for conscience. She came down from the loft and went to get a spade.

On her way out, the implement over her shoulder, she checked in with Arthur. He was on the verge of his afternoon nap. She wondered, distantly, what an invasion of all that was impossible would mean for him. "What would you do tonight," she asked him, "if you were me?"

"Stay home and look after me, you old cow."

"Right. Now I know what not to do." Before he could

start to yell, she was out the door and heading for the woods.

Autumn had felt that the most obvious way to learn about the Sovo symbol was to experiment on the one on her own door. She used every incantation and aid to focus she knew about, now with, she had to admit, an added expectation that they might have results in the physical world. Nothing changed the marking. She tried to cool it, using everything from ice to fragrances that suggested winter. Nothing worked. She had a sudden thought of corporate espionage, hacking into Sovo's computer, like in the movies, though she didn't know anyone who could do that, and looked up where the label said the paint was made, but it turned out to be somewhere in Taiwan, with a website that defied Google translation. The ingredients listed on the tin were reasonably rare: amaranth, Spanish Moss, mullein, valerian root, vetivert . . . you could find galangal in Waitrose, and a few of the others in Holland & Barrett, but most of them in processed form, not the originals that the recipe seemed to demand. In parts of the United States you could go out and pick Spanish moss, but that wasn't true in Britain. Still, the Internet would bring everything to one's door.

She checked her ingredient wholesalers online, and found to her surprise that supplies of several of the herbs had been reduced to zero, with the red "reordering, more soon" lettering beside the checkboxes. She made a couple of calls and found that bulk purchasers had raided all the major depots. Would Sovo really need that much of this stuff to daub even every door in one small town? It wasn't like they were doing this all over the country. Judith had gone on about how unique Lychford was. She checked her own shelves: there were only small amounts of a few of the relevant ingredients.

Then she realised. All those new customers in the last couple of weeks, all seeming to want the ability to vanish. They hadn't been here as individual shoppers, they'd been Sovo workers, buying up her stock to write invisible signs on doors. She slumped on the work bench, annoyed at how that had gotten past her, but then a new thought came to her. Sovo didn't need this stuff themselves. They just didn't want anyone else having it. Which meant there must be some way it could be used against them.

She went to the paint pot, and found almost nothing left in it. She'd used up a lot of it in her experiments. Still, it didn't matter how much she had if she didn't know what to do with it. The idea of what she could actually do, and the idea of where she might get the ingredients to do it came together in her mind in one terrible moment. She had to put a hand onto the bench to support herself. How could she even be contemplating this?

Judith had said this working, whatever it was, had required sacrifice. So sacrifice could be used against it. There was an obvious sacrifice she could make.

If she was going to do it, it had to be done today. She didn't see she had a choice. She pulled on her coat and headed for the door, and after she'd locked up, she called Judith and then Lizzie and left messages, sharing her discoveries and her plan. It was possible she wouldn't see either of them again.

6

Judith found the place in the woods surprisingly quickly. Every tree had its history visible, and golden threads of information shone between them, leading her down the years to her memories. He'd been so beautiful. Ridiculous. Nasty. Spouting such bollocks. He'd told her he loved her and she'd just said that must be great. He didn't get the words he was after, but she didn't leave him with anything to complain about. Or so she'd thought. He'd stormed off, and it was only later, when she met Arthur, she'd discovered the curse he'd placed on her, what she'd lived with ever since. That had made her how she was, she supposed, if that was how personalities really worked.

She found the place they'd buried the squirrel. It was still a black pit in the world of her greater senses, still stank of contamination. She'd protected herself with silver, dabbed on her wrists, but to her eyes a halo of shining armour. She dug hard and swiftly, her old body screaming at her, her willpower letting her ignore it.

She found the squirrel. It was a skeleton, but it was still being killed by what Robin had infested it with from that twig. It hissed its little skeletal mouth at her, in torment. She harvested the black tarlike stuff with a spoon from the back of her cutlery drawer, one she was willing to throw out, and gathered it into a velvet bag that squealed and squirmed in her hands. Then she contained the velvet in several ziplock sandwich bags and was finally satisfied that death couldn't escape.

She gave the squirrel all the peace she could with water and words of release, but still couldn't quiet it. She hadn't expected to be rid of her old sins that easily. She covered it again with earth as swiftly as she could, and, propped up by her stick, headed home with her awful prize.

She wondered, as she often had, what had become of Robin. Those who played with such magic usually got eaten by it. She stopped at the signpost that indicated the way back to Lychford and read the sign which Autumn hadn't been able to make out on the way to the well: *All Other Routes*. All of them, they had that right.

She realised there was something standing in the bushes nearby, and turned to look at it. It was the thing that had killed Eric Parker—that had also been the wisp that had first tried the town's defences. It was now fully formed, a silhouette of a man, a pit in human form, a whole demon. It smelled of piss and broken promises.

Judith prepared herself for it to attack, but instead it

simply raised an arm and indicated she should proceed. From the bushes around it stepped many others of its kind.

They were biding their time, she realised. They could afford to wait. Sometime after 7 P.M. tonight they'd be able to walk into Lychford and harvest as they pleased.

Unless Judith could bring herself to do a terrible thing.

Autumn had never before felt such fear as on that early afternoon, as she ventured into the woods. She hadn't gone by the paths Judith had shown them, but into the parts of the forest she remembered mainly because she'd taken care never to go back there. With her new senses, it felt even more like she was stepping into a nightmare. The forest loomed over her and confirmed with every stride that she was deliberately walking back into what had destroyed her life.

She found herself fighting to stop jogging downhill, her boots slipping on the carpet of decaying leaves, as, after a point, every angle of the forest floor led to what was ahead. She fell just as she saw it and scrambled back onto her feet. Here was what those without her new senses could never find. Across two stark and leafless trees was hung a garland of blossoming flowers. In the gap between the trees it was summer. Blue sky shone there, and here was the smell of heat and nature that took her stomach right back there, and ... oh, God, there it was, very quietly, that music.

She made herself walk right up to the edge of it, feeling the volume increase as pressure fell away in her ears, as if she were taking off in an aircraft. She could see, over the low garland, lost in a summer mist, the shapes of buildings beyond. She knew what lay inside those buildings. She knew the way back to the centre of her nightmare. "Finn!" she called.

No reply.

She was sure, with her new senses, that he must have heard her. She'd felt that shout connect. She knew what he wanted her to do, what she had to do if she was going to save everything. "Let me come back with enough time to do it," she said, and she didn't know who to, maybe to Lizzie, to the higher love Lizzie represented. "Let me come back." And she stepped, of her own free will, over the border.

———————

Lizzie spent the afternoon going round the pubs, in her collar, gauging opinion. She saw Autumn had left a voicemail on her phone, but when she listened to it, it was just static that, to her new hearing, seemed to have a mocking tone to it. The sound of it chilled her. Had they done something to harm Autumn? The Sovo workers had taken up a corner in the Railway, and were politely declining offers of drinks and ignoring punters who wanted to have a go at them. The meeting was due to start at 7 P.M.

Lizzie went and stood on the steps of the town hall as people headed in, the whole town, it looked like, including those she knew were planning to vote against, a bleak-looking Mrs. Parker, in the midst of her grief, among them. So the symbols on the doors hadn't stopped them leaving their houses or, so far, done them harm.

Suddenly, she saw Judith. The old lady had a forlorn look on her face, shaking her head at whatever her son, walking beside her in uniform, was trying to say to her. Lizzie arrived as he left to resume his post as crowd control. "Why haven't you called? Isn't there anything we can do? Have you seen Autumn?"

Judith licked her lips, moistening them against the cold. She seemed not to want to meet Lizzie's gaze. "I got a message from her, which I couldn't hear. They'd done something to erase it."

"Judith, what's wrong?"

"Forgive me, Mother, for I have sinned."

"Okay . . . but we really should do this in private—"

She finally looked at her, with some of her old wryness. "I wasn't talking to you."

"What's going on? What's the plan?"

"I'm going to do the only thing I can do, and you mustn't have anything to do with it."

Lizzie grabbed her arm. "I'm not going to step away. Not after all you've shown me."

Judith looked angry, but then a sad smile appeared on her face. "On your own head be it, Reverend."

———————

Maureen Crewdson sat on stage and made herself watch as everyone she knew in town, everyone she didn't know, perhaps everybody, filed into the hall, and filled every corner of it. The local media, such as they were, had turned out—a couple of reporters and someone from Radio Gloucestershire carrying a microphone. Even the teenagers who sat on the roundabout at the park were here, presumably lured by the possibility of violent conflict. Or perhaps this was all Sovo's doing. Mr. Cummings had smiled when he said he expected a big turnout. When Maureen had become mayor it had seemed like a reasonably fun thing for a community-minded person to take on. All she had to do, she thought, was keep her sensible hat on, and the challenges were all issues she knew very well from her voluntary work. Then Sovo had arrived.

She had genuinely been onside at first, and so when David Cummings had offered to pay her "expenses," which had sorted her worries about keeping her old mum in the care home she liked, she'd only hesitated a moment: she was being paid to support a cause she supported anyway. They could waste their money on her if they liked. This was obviously just how grown-ups did things.

However, as it became clear the issue was tearing the town apart, she'd started to have her doubts. She'd started to worry about how she could tell those in the anti camp that she was listening to them when she'd been paid not to.

When she put some difficult questions to Cummings, he'd said they had to be very careful who knew about the bribe. He'd actually used that word. If people gossiped, he'd said, she could lose her job, even go to prison, and what would happen to her mum then?

She'd gradually become sure that word had gotten out, that people were gossiping, from the looks on the faces of her former friends, and her colleagues in the town council. The last straw had been when Judith Maw-son—her neighbour, who everyone thought of as this rude old battleaxe with mental health issues, but who had started knocking on Maureen's door when Maureen's husband had died—had suddenly gotten that awful look on her face. Now here Maureen was, trying to keep a calm expression, while everyone who hated her sat down in front of her and waited for her to be the Judas they expected her to be. It wasn't as if the other side loved her for what she'd done either.

Beside her, she felt David Cummings sit down. She knew he was smiling. She didn't turn to look.

She watched as Judith entered, the new vicar with her. The reverend seemed to be urgently asking her about something, with such a fearful expression—not something you ever saw on a vicar. She was obviously horrified about whatever Judith had told her. That terrible look on Judith's face too. All the horror of this moment, she was wearing it. Sunil had come in at the other end of the hall, looking around for Judith and failing to find her. She wished desperately that those two might find some happiness, that at least she'd done some good trying to bring them together. Two rows back, there was Sheila Parker, already crying, comforted by supporters who were glaring at Maureen, as if Eric Parker's death was her fault too. She had to look away. She had to run this meeting the way Cummings had told her to, had to let all the other bribes he'd doubtless made have their influence, had to keep up the pretence of democracy. She had no way out. She got to her feet.

"Everyone," she began, "thank you for coming. If you look around you, I don't think we're missing anyone with an interest in this matter. Does anyone know anyone who hasn't got here yet, who ought to be here?" This was the wording Cummings had insisted on.

"My Eric!" shouted Sheila Parker, and there was applause.

It took Maureen a moment before she could continue. She ran through the usual business of a council meeting, with thankfully nothing much in the way of reports or other motions, the councillors having for once realised the crowd would get restive if someone started grandstanding about drainage at the cricket club. Finally, they got to the matter at hand. "Since we're all here, I have to tell you, the council have been having a series of ... sometimes fraught ... meetings about the matter of Sovo building a store here." Cheers and yells. "It's time for the vote, though I think I know which way it's going to go." She read out the official wording of the proposal and asked for a show of hands for those in favour. Six of the twelve councillors on stage beside her raised theirs. She took a deep breath. "The council are divided equally, so the deciding vote comes down to ... me." There was, as Cummings had told her there would be, a roar of disapproval. She talked over it, kept saying it until they listened. "But I don't want to make my . . . my choice overrule the will of the people of this town. Okay?" They were listening now; this was odd. "Since everyone's here, I'm going to ask all of *you* to vote, a simple show of hands, and I'm going to cast my vote with whichever side has the majority. I hope in so doing I will put an end to the conflict that's done us . . . done us so much damage." They gradually started to make approving noises. They thought that was fair. Of course they did. That was the plan. She risked a glance across to Cummings. He was acting, doing his best to look shocked, his fingers making nervous shapes at high speed. How many of this audience had he bribed? How could he be so sure the knife-edge vote wouldn't go against him?

———————

Judith nudged Lizzie in the ribs and whispered, "Look what he's doing with his fingers. Can you feel it? Whatever he's planning with those symbols on the doors, it's happening now."

Lizzie could feel it. Something was gripping the room, coming and going in waves. She realised she was seeing the rhythm as she felt it, to the same rhythm as Cummings moved his fingers. She could feel it in herself, too, a little intrusion in her gut with every flex, that was moving its way up her shoulder, making the top of her arm twitch, a feeling of pins and needles gripping her, and with the feeling that her arm wanted to move, a feeling that she genuinely wanted to move that arm, because she genuinely wanted to vote, to vote for . . . "He's using the symbols to control the vote," she said.

"As simple as that," said Judith, sounding oddly calm. "Look around, he's doing it to about half those who were going to vote against. It's all he needs."

"I hope that now you can see you're free to choose." Cummings had got to his feet, still flexing his fingers, as if nervous. "You'll see that voting for our store will bring the community together again." He sat down, and one of the councillors got up to make the case against, but Lizzie could see even she was rubbing at her arm, feeling the same thing many of those against did.

"I have to do it now," said Judith as the councillor finished speaking, a great sadness in her voice. "I'm sorry." Before Lizzie could stop her, she was on her feet, and had pulled from the pocket of her coat a blackened twig, which to Lizzie now looked like the most terrifying thing she had ever seen. Judith pointed it at Cummings. "Out out out, death to you, death!" she screamed.

Lizzie tried to grab the twig from her, certain as she did so that touching it would harm her hands, but Judith pushed her aside and sent her sprawling into the aisle. As the audience yelled and screamed—obviously thinking Judith had some sort of weapon—Lizzie felt the horrible potential of the twig suddenly release itself. For a moment she was sure she could see it, a jagged rip of blackness that consumed the world between Judith and Cummings, murder thrown at him from what had immediately become Judith's hopelessly blackened heart, the short circuit of hatred bringing a stench that burst across the hall. Lizzie was aghast. Whatever they thought Cummings was, he was also a person, with a real wife and children. She hauled herself to her feet and stared . . . at Cummings raising a bemused eyebrow.

The audience had turned to Judith, some shouting their anger, some now laughing in relief and mockery, some still crying out in fear. She lowered the twig, a confused, desperate expression on her face, a helpless old woman.

Lizzie took Judith's arm and tried to steady her as she rocked on her feet. She could see she was crying, her fingers numbly still trying to extract an ounce more hatred from what had become just a twig. As Lizzie watched, the wood crumbled in her fingers. Judith curled over, weeping, and sat down.

Lizzie could only sit beside her, horrified. That had been their last chance. Where the hell was Autumn? Had she run away?

"Well . . . ," the mayor, looking ashen, took a moment to bring the meeting to order, glancing in their direction then away again. "Let's . . . let's go ahead and have that vote, then . . ."

Lizzie desperately wondered if she could make any difference with some sort of speech, at least delay things. Suddenly, she heard a welcome, familiar voice from someone who'd sat down beside her. "Let it happen." She turned to see Autumn, a calm, serious look on her face. Lizzie opened her mouth to protest, but Autumn shook her head. She looked changed, somehow . . . no, she looked more like the Autumn she'd first known: grounded, strong. Lizzie looked to Judith and saw that the old woman was blinking, wondering where Autumn had found such hope.

"All those in favour?" said Maureen.

Lizzie grabbed her own arm, relieved she was able to use her willpower to do that, and feeling . . . actually no urge to raise her hand. The sensation in her arm had remained there, failing to move her arm as if the muscles were too exhausted to carry a weight. She looked around the room. About half of those present had raised their hands, the ones who'd supported Sovo. Some who had previously were keeping their hands down, one or two of those who'd been against had their hands up. It was what you might expect from a free vote. She looked to Cummings, who was staring at the audience in genuine shock now, his fingers working feverishly, fury starting to show on his features.

"Oh," said Judith, her hand over her mouth in relief and amazement. "Oh."

"I tied the knot to activate it," said Autumn, "just before I walked in. Sorry to leave it so late." She held up a sprig of some sort of herb, knotted and daubed with red paint.

Maureen finished doing a head count and checked with the councillors and the secretary that they all agreed with the number. "And those against?"

Another free show of hands. Lizzie put hers up, as did Autumn, a proud grin on her face, and Judith, astonished. About half the room joined them. There was more counting, which led to a whispered debate on stage. Finally, Maureen looked up from the notepads. "It's a tie," she said.

"That's . . . that's impossible," said Cummings. Lizzie was delighted to hear those words from him.

"So it really is down to me," said the mayor. The room became angry again. Lizzie realised that if what she'd heard about Maureen was true, then they were going to lose anyway. Cummings had obviously realised that too, looking urgently to her. Maureen didn't meet his gaze.

She was instead making eye contact with Judith, who was blinking back tears, urging her on. "I . . . I've hated the way this debate has ripped us apart. You all know . . . I took their money." There were gasps from the crowd, then angry shouts. Cummings was staring at her. Judith smiled, amazed as if she couldn't believe in this much good. "My friend Judith . . . you just saw what this has done to her. It's been stressful for all of us, but it's sent her over the edge, and . . . and I just can't stand it anymore. I vote against."

The crowd leapt up around Lizzie, Autumn, and Judith, a roar of triumph blotting out anything Lizzie might have wanted to say. She grabbed Autumn, and they held each other. After a moment, they looked to Judith. The smile had faded. She was looking extremely offended.

———————

While the townspeople in the hall were still celebrating, commiserating, and debating, and Shaun was asking Maureen urgent questions, in answer to which she was sadly nodding, Autumn led them out of the hall. "I risk my soul, or whatever you want to call it," Judith was saying, "with forbidden magics, and she thinks I've gone doolally!"

Lizzie saw Cummings, flanked by Sovo workers, leaving the hall at speed, hoping to avoid the local media. He was stumbling, limping, waving away employees who were trying to offer him assistance. It almost looked like he'd been physically harmed. "I'd prefer to say that she felt sympathy for you and that pricked her conscience."

Judith just glared at her, then looked to Autumn. "What did you do?"

Autumn led them to a door in the Market Place, a coffee shop that was home to a couple who'd been against Sovo. The symbol still burned bright, but now it was different, Lizzie saw, the triangle having been turned into a pentagram. Autumn took a coffee jar full of paint from her coat pocket. "You were right, Judith. The shape of the symbol was the important thing. We couldn't erase them, or paint over them, but with enough of the right sort of paint, I added to them. I made them into this." She held up the symbol on her necklace. "It takes doing. Four more triangles on each and a fiddly bit in the middle. Some of them went really wrong. I'm glad that didn't, you know, turn anyone into anything."

"A manipulation," said Judith. "You found a way."

"Where did you get the paint and that herb knot thing?" asked Lizzie.

"From us," said a voice nearby. They all turned to see what Lizzie took to be Finn, clad not very sensibly in a vest and jeans, his breath not visible on the air like theirs were. He was also holding a pot of paint and a brush. "I helped."

"Is that him?" asked Lizzie.

"Oh, thank God, you can see him," said Autumn.

"Bloody fairies," said Judith. "You went to the lands again, then?"

"I went to see his father," said Autumn, and there was again a tremor in her voice. "I apologised for offending him. I . . . managed to look at him. He replied, and his voice was . . . I didn't understand what he said."

Finn sighed. "He accepted your sacrifice of fear."

"And you made a sacrifice," said Judith, "having appealed to a higher power. It took all three."

"I'm not clear on what happened after that. Things went into a kind of blur. I think something happened with time."

"Dad," said Finn, "had all the Summerland gather what you needed and sent you back to be his sword and shield and save the way of the worlds and made sure you arrived back way before the meeting started, and sent me with you to do the bit with the doors in record time, without anyone seeing."

"Yeah," said Autumn, "I thought it must be something like that."

"I have to report back," said Finn. "Will I see you

again?"

"Maybe."

"Annoying. But also . . . excellent. Nobody ever plays hard to get." He walked into a shadow and after a moment Lizzie realised he wasn't there anymore.

"So," she said, "that's a fairy."

"Yeah," whispered Autumn.

"He didn't look like a fairy."

"What were you expecting?"

"For him to look like a fairy."

Judith looked to Autumn and sized her up for a moment before finally nodding. "That was . . . all right." She paused for a moment and seemed to decide on something. "I'm not getting any younger. Despite everything I've tried. You two . . . you're not on my list of what I don't like. The great powers find failure in their incarnations very hard to deal with. They tend to withdraw their influence, leaving their human forms a bit ill and angry, but you know what it's like dealing with a dying wasp. He might well have another go. Or sneak in to cause havoc in some other way. And other things in the darkness out there, things like I've met recently, might have seen how shaky the walls of Lychford are getting, and right now will be thinking about having a go, whether or not they've got Cummings to help them. If you two are willing, perhaps it's time for me to take on an apprentice, and to take more seriously the traditional relationship between the local wise woman and the clergy."

"Are you saying you could use our help?" said Autumn.

"Don't push it."

"Because I was going to say I could use your help in the shop."

"Your wisdom, she means," said Lizzie. "To make the shop into what it needs to be."

Judith glowered, but held out her hand, then looked away and almost imperceptibly nodded as Lizzie and then Autumn took it. After a second, she shook away their touch. "Lychford is going to need us," she said.

"The only thing is," said Lizzie, "I'm not sure what good I'll be to you. I . . ." She was going to say that nowhere in all this had she found her faith. Cummings was certainly some sort of evil supernatural power, but that didn't seem to imply to her the presence of a God, any more than it did in the movies. Looking at Autumn's ill-concealed pleasure, however, she didn't feel like raining on her parade. "I . . . didn't do anything to help."

Judith actually smiled. "You will," she said quietly. Then, declining Lizzie's offer of help, she pushed off with her stick and marched off unsteadily towards her home.

———————

Autumn and Lizzie ended up in the Plough, where a number of those from the meeting had congregated. From what Lizzie could overhear, it seemed shared jokes about the mayor's confession and Judith's eccentricity were starting to once more pull the town together.

"What were you trying to tell me earlier?" asked Autumn.

So Lizzie, haltingly at first, proceeded to tell her at first just about Joe, but then, unable to stop herself, about everything.

"Oh," said Autumn. "Oh, no." She took Lizzie's hands in her own. "I'm sorry I wasn't there for you. And . . . I'm sorry you're having a wobble about your faith."

"Really?"

"Yeah. I got to find out how real my impossible beings were. I even got to show them to other people. But you—"

"That's something I'd have gone through even if all this hadn't happened."

"We should catch up. We should catch up right now," decided Autumn. "Until closing time."

She was pleasingly shocked when Lizzie took off her collar.

Judith made her way slowly back to her house, feeling the exhaustion brought on by using the dark stuff. She'd only done it twice before in her whole life. The sense of potency it gave you . . . well, she could see why it was so addictive. That was why Robin had turned out to be someone who could do . . . what he'd done to her. She might have known, though, that Cummings would have been immune to her ultimate weapon. That darkness was what he breathed.

"Judith!" The voice as she reached for her keys made her jump, but it was just Sunil, catching up with her. "I tried to find you after the meeting—"

Judith didn't want to deal with this now. Her being so shaken up, she felt like she might give in to how she felt about him. "I'm sorry, I'm very tired."

"But you're all right?"

"Not quite gibbering, if that's what you mean."

He took her hand. She felt how cold her hand was in his. "I know you believe in this. And so, I'm guessing what you did back there was pretty extreme. Judith, come back with me, let me get you some food, sit by my fire. Don't go into that cold house all alone."

She looked to the upstairs window, and saw the light

of Arthur's television. She was so tempted. "I can't."

"It's your husband, isn't it?"

"Yes," she whispered.

"Judith, I know Arthur was your whole world. He was my friend too. But it's been ten years since he died, ten years since the funeral."

"I know," she said quietly. She let go of his hand, and he let her, and she didn't look at him again, but instead went inside and closed the door behind her.

Epilogue

That Sunday, despite a hangover which had lasted all of yesterday, Lizzie got to her church early and unlocked everything and lit the candles with half an hour to go before the early service. She was now, she realised as she stood looking towards the altar, a priest who believed in fairies but wasn't sure if she believed in God. She could feel the gravity of this building, the way it was connected to everything, and that felt good, but there was still nothing beyond that. She went to the flowers that stood in front of the old map on the wall and moved them out of the way. People would ask questions. That was good.

She was now also friends, once again, with the town's most obvious pagan. That was a friendship that was going to cause fewer mutterings in the congregation than one might expect. Anglicans were, when it came down to it, generally tolerant types with ecumenical interests. Having Autumn back in her life was a source of great joy. Joy enough to make up for the damage it was going to do to her liver. She missed a greater joy, though. She missed it very much and wondered if having Autumn around might somehow prevent her from ever finding it again.

She went to the organ stool and found once again the hidden collection plate, still with the money on it. She lifted it out. She'd have a big congregation coming in later this morning for the main service. She didn't feel like hiding anything now. So, what was she going to do with this money?

She felt the presence of him beside her, and turned, quite calmly in the circumstances, to find him there. "Mr. Cummings."

He looked rough around the edges, like he'd slept in his suit. Even with her new senses, she still couldn't feel anything strange about him. She couldn't now, though, quite imagine him going back to one of the hotels on the ring road. "Do the poor know you allow yourself such luxury?" he said, pointing to the collection plate. He sounded a little desperate. He stumbled, had to grab at a pew to hold himself up, and as he did so, he let a little of his remaining power show. It was like hearing distant thunder. The size of it made Lizzie gasp and take a step back. She was suddenly scared for herself, if not for her town. It felt to her now like this wounded beast might do anything.

"What luxury?"

"Doubt. Why haven't you taken that?"

Now she had an answer. "Because I'd owe you something."

"Oh, come on now. When you think I'm . . . whatever you think I am? You still feel you'd have to repay me? "

After everything that had happened, why had he chosen to come back here? What did he want with her? She failed to speak, and then managed it, not quite knowing from where inside her the word came. "Yes."

"But I want to do something good! Please, just this one small thing. I hereby declare to whoever is listening that I will not seek any recompense for you taking that money. No bargains. Nothing. It is a gift."

She was almost crying again, and she had no idea why. "You just want me to do what you tell me."

He was suddenly yelling. "It's not *my* ego that's the problem here! Lizzie, if you asked anyone in your congregation, they'd say take that money and give it to the poor. What else are you *for*? What else is the institution you belong to for, if not to walk the walk rather than all the talk talk talk? That's what you've said yourself in the past, though it seems you didn't mean it. It would be laughing in my face now for you to take that money. Joe would have wanted you to *take that money*."

Lizzie made herself meet his gaze, and suddenly realised that in it she'd found everything she needed. She went and grabbed a candle and before he could say anything else she thrust the flame into the bundle of notes.

It burst into flame, perhaps more quickly and more powerfully than money should? She wasn't sure. She'd never seen money burn before.

Cummings began a slow handclap. "Oh well done. Bravo! Wait until the newspapers hear. What *is* the Church of England coming to?"

"I'll find the money myself. Every penny."

"That's the spirit! How long do you think that'll take you? Until you retire? Not even then?" He stepped forward, into her face, smiling an enormous, desperate, demanding smile. "I could pop back every now and then, offer you some useful ways of making extra cash. What do you say?"

"I say . . ." Lizzie put her fingers to the crucifix on her necklace. "Though I walk through the valley of the shadow of death, I will fear no evil."

He didn't hiss like a vampire in a movie. He stumbled back a couple of steps. He looked at her like a child who'd had his magic trick spoiled. "Well," he muttered, "now you know." Suddenly, he was gone. He just wasn't there anymore. He left a slight smell of dust in the air. It felt to Lizzie like something had finally fallen apart.

Lizzie blinked. She took a hesitant step forward into the space where he'd been. She found she had inside her a feeling she'd misplaced for so long. In a moment, she would go and kneel. She looked back to the plate where all that remained of the money was ashes. Her heart sank at the sight, but now there was only so far it could sink. "We'll hold a bingo night," she whispered. "An enormous bingo night."

―――――――――

In the early afternoon, Lizzie got back to the vicarage, having preached a couple of—perhaps a bit too emotional—sermons, the personal aspects of which had made the churchwardens raise an eyebrow. She was going to have to have a word with them, to find out the details of what they'd found too unbelievable to tell. "Well," Sue had said as she was tidying up the church, "you've got into your stride. Finally." Lizzie found the letter she'd written to the bishop, ripped it up, and threw the pieces into the bin. She needed to tell Judith and Autumn about Cummings.

Later for that. She went and flopped onto the sofa, exhausted. She allowed her thoughts to drift, and she fell asleep in the low light of the autumn afternoon and dreamed, as she'd expected to, of Joe. They walked again in the sunshine beside that deadly road. "You wanted me to give that money to the poor," she said.

"You *never* bloody did what I said."

"I've gotten my faith back, and more. There's even

more to the universe than I thought there was."

"Brilliant."

"Goodbye, Joe," she said.

About the Author

© Lou Abercrombie, 2015

Paul Cornell is a writer of science fiction and fantasy in prose, comics, and television, one of only two people to be Hugo Award nominated for all three media. A *New York Times* #1 bestselling author, he's written *Doctor Who* for the BBC, *Wolverine* for Marvel, and *Batman & Robin* for DC. He's won the BSFA Award for his short fiction, an Eagle Award for his comics, and shares in a Writer's Guild Award for his TV work.

TOR·COM

Science fiction. Fantasy.
The universe.
And related subjects.

★

More than just a publisher's website, Tor.com
is a venue for **original fiction, comics,** and
discussion of the entire field of SF and fantasy,
in all media and from all sources. Visit our site
today—and join the conversation yourself.